Destiny, Valor,
and a lizard named
Louie

Michael Ambrosio

Illustrations by Bob Langan

LionX Publishing
Folsom ❖ California

LionX Publishing, Inc.
705-2 East Bidwell Street, Suite #235
Folsom, Ca. 95630-3315

First Edition
Printed in the United States of America.
9 8 7 6 5 4 3 2 1

Dedicated to my good friend who really doesn't look like a lizard at all.

Special thanks to Judy Schuler, Heartland Reviews for her editing inputs.
Extra special thanks to Carla, (the best teacher in the world), for the study guide,
Ryan for his final edit checks, Drew for his picture placement advice, and to
Alisa for her administrative help.

"In the day when I cried out, You answered me,
And made me bold with strength in my soul." Ps 138:3

Publisher's Cataloging-in-Publication Data
(Prepared by The Donohue Group, Inc.)

Ambrosio, Michael.
   Destiny, valor, and a lizard named Louie / Michael Ambrosio ; illustrated by
Bob Langan. -- [1st ed.]
      p. cm.
   ISBN: 0-9716085-3-9 (pbk.)
1. Lizards--Juvenile fiction. 2. Chameleons--Juvenile fiction. I. Langan, Bob. II.
Title. III. Title: Destiny, valor, & a lizard named Louie.

PS3551.M25 D47 2004
813/.54--dc21

Publication Date: March 2004

Visit us on the World Wide Web
www.lionxpublishing.com

CONTENTS

Chapter

"The lizard you may grasp with the hands,
Yet it is in kings' palaces."
Ancient Proverb

CHAPTER 1

ANGRY KOMODO DRAGON

Outnumbered and surrounded, the King's blue-belly lizards fought bravely. They had been ambushed in a terrible turn of events. Their enemies, the chameleons, knew they were no match for King Scelo and his blue-belly army, so they turned to deception[1]. Masters of color change and disguise, the chameleons had convinced the island's only remaining monitor lizard, Komo, that King Scelo was his enemy.

Fooled by the chameleon's lies, Komo came upon King Scelo's troops from behind. The lizards could not hold out against Komo; he was squashing five and ten lizards at a time under his clawed feet.

"We have to fight through them," King Scelo commanded. He and his top commander, Talis, rallied the army to fight through to the hilltop at their right.

The chameleons fought hard. They knew, if they just held their ground, Komo would eventually come through. Nevertheless, little by little, the lizards fought their way to the hilltop.

"Form a circle around the King," Talis shouted. The courageous blue-bellies did their best. The chameleons couldn't break through.

The chameleon general, Cramstack, yelled for Komo. "Take that hill and you'll have your revenge! The King is up there!"

---

[1] deception – to deceive; the telling of a lie to get what you want

Komo turned.

With the large monitor lizard approaching the hill, King Scelo turned to his commander. "Talis, take ten of your best soldiers, fight your way down the backside of this hill and get to the castle. Take the prince and move him to safety. Now!"

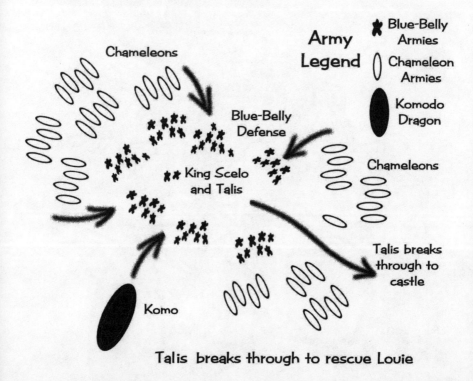

Talis breaks through to rescue Louie

Talis knew this was it; he would never see his King again. Talis hesitated to leave the King he had so faithfully served for all these years.

Their eyes met. King Scelo knew what his commander was thinking. His training was to protect the King at all costs. What he was asking Talis to do went against every instinct his commander had ever known. "Do it for me. Do it for the future of our kind, do it now, hurry," King Scelo said softly. With the love of a father in his eyes, he put his hands on Talis' shoulders. "Tell my son I love him."

With steely eyes, Talis saluted his King. He quickly picked ten soldiers and began fighting his way through the chameleon force on the other side of the hill.

Meanwhile, Komo was at the base of the hill. "Today you will pay with your life and your kingdom!" Komo shouted.

Komo has been confused by the chameleon's lies; I must find a way to get through to him, King Scelo thought.

"What is your complaint, my old ally and friend," King Scelo shouted back.

"You know what you have done! Don't play dumb with me!" Komo fumed. "Your assassins killed my son, and now I'm the only monitor lizard left. You broke the treaty, my trust, and our friendship. All to make sure your son would rule this island unchallenged. Your evil will be judged this day!"

"But those were not my assassins," King Scelo

replied.

"They had your royal seal!" Komo exclaimed.

Oh those chameleons are good, the King thought. *How can I get Komo to see the truth? His son is dead and he believes I did it.*

Komo began up the hill, crushing blue-belly warriors beneath his feet. Anger and pain in his eyes, he was moments from reaching the King.

What can I say to convince him? The King's thoughts raced as he watched his own warrior's futile attempt to hold Komo back.

Komo's large clawed foot came down swiftly, pinning King Scelo on the ground. "I will crush you slowly, painfully," Komo seethed.

King Scelo, gasping for air, saw it. In a moment, in a vision flashing through his mind; assassins coming in at night, catching the young monitor lizard asleep. *The tails, that's it!* King Scelo tried for one good breath, "The tails, did you see the assassins tails?"

"What?" Komo paused. He let up a little on the King.

"The tails, did you catch a glimpse of the assassins tails?" King Scelo cried.

"They came in too fast and left even faster. Yes, I saw their tails, lizards, with curled tails." Komo was confused.

"We blue-bellies have straight tails, look around you. Chameleons have curled tails, they stole my royal seal and made it look like we did it. But we have always been your friends and allies. I would not break your trust. We are not liars like the chameleons."

Komo began to feel sick. But the chameleon general had seen and heard too much. Cramstack had hidden some of his best troops in the tree on the hilltop. With a single command, these chameleons pounced on the monitor lizard and began stabbing him with their little swords.

Overcome by the sheer number of chameleons, Komo fell to the ground. "I'm so sorry, so sorry," he breathed. "I didn't know."

King Scelo, crippled and near death himself, shouted to his remaining troops, "Retreat! Retreat!" Then the chameleons quickly overcame him as darkness fell.

CHAPTER 2

NEW PLANS

Too exhausted to notice their wounds, Talis and his remaining three soldiers ran to the castle gate. "Let us in! Let us in! By command of the King!"

The gate guards barely recognizing Talis, opened the drawbridge. He stumbled inside and called for Prince Louie. The wall guard ran to get the prince, who was only three years old.

What could the prince understand at his age? How could Talis explain all that had happened and all that it would mean? The time for explaining would have to come later. For now Talis had to move Louie out of the castle, but where?

"The chameleons will be coming soon. We don't have the troops to defeat them. Take the prince and some supplies, we will head for the forest," Talis commanded.

The small group of soldiers guarding the castle packed some supplies and with the prince, headed for the forest. Once inside the cover of the woods, Talis felt a little safer. They stopped beside a riverbank to rest and plan their next move. Talis was exhausted.

The King is surely dead by now and General Cramstack and his chameleon forces are no doubt overrunning the land. Chameleon forces with a monitor lizard as their main weapon. Talis winced at the thought. *No blue-belly lizard is a match against a monitor.*

Suddenly Talis became aware of movement in the forest. *Oh, no. Have the chameleons caught up with us so soon?* Talis worried.

But from behind some bushes came a tattered soldier. "Commander, commander, I found you!" the soldier muttered. "Request permission to report, sir," he said more clearly.

"Report soldier," replied Talis, not really wanting to hear the bad news.

"The King...the King is dead. Our army is in retreat as the King commanded."

"How many soldiers left?" Talis asked.

"A few, sir. After the King commanded the retreat, the chameleons backed off. Probably because they didn't have the monitor lizard anymore."

Talis was shocked. "They don't have the monitor lizard?"

"That's right, the King must have gotten through to him because the chameleons killed him right before they killed...before they killed the King," the soldier said somberly.

Talis had a glimmer of hope. With the chameleons left to themselves they had a chance. But then he also realized that most of the army was already crushed by the huge lizard. *I need a plan,* he thought. *The King is dead. Any soldiers I find will be looking to me, at least until Louie is old enough to lead. I need wisdom, the wisdom of a king.*

Later that day, after nursing their wounds and collecting a few more stragglers, Talis laid out his plan.

Talking to his soldiers, Talis explained. "First we need to build a base deep inside the forest. This will enable us to start rebuilding our forces and keep us safe from the chameleons, in case they come trying to find us. Chameleons are cowards at heart. If we use the forest as cover, they will be very unwilling to come in and get us."

"But how will we rebuild our forces?" one soldier asked.

"The chameleons are fewer in number than the lizard folk. So I believe they won't kill the peasants. They'll probably use them as slave labor and keep them alive. So from time to time we will sneak into the villages and get young male lizards around fifteen years old, take them back into the forest and train them," Talis replied.

"Ah, and with them, we will slowly rebuild our army," the soldier observed.

"Yes! And when the time is right, we will reclaim this land in the name of the King and free the com-

mon lizards from the chameleon cruelty!" Talis
exclaimed, feeling more hopeful as he heard the
words coming through his own lips.

"This sounds like a good plan commander, but
our King is dead, so..." replied another soldier.

"You're forgetting the Prince," Talis quickly
interrupted. "We'll have to find a good peasant family,
one near the edge of the forest so we can keep a
watchful eye on him. We'll ask this family to take
Louie as their own. He'll have to blend in as a peasant. He's so young, that shouldn't be too difficult.
Then when he's old enough, we'll take him into the
forest, train him as a soldier and as our new King."

"But what if Louie forgets who he is? I mean he is only three. How much will he remember of his father, of being a King, of being a good King?" the soldier questioned.

"That's a risk," Talis admitted. "But we have no other choice. We must trust that Louie will be ready when it's time."

And with that, the blue-belly lizards that had survived began to put their long and careful plans into place.

Meanwhile, looking over the newly captured castle grounds, General Cramstack was very pleased with himself. King Scelo was dead, the blue-belly army almost completely destroyed, and the land was his for the taking.

"We can't find the prince anywhere," reported the chameleon soldier.

"It's not important now," replied General Cramstack, rubbing his hands together. The chameleon general had a plan of his own.

Gathering his chief leaders together, General Cramstack gave his directions. "Congratulations soldiers, the island is ours! Now I want you to take the villages that have been assigned to you. Don't kill the blue-belly peasants, unless you absolutely have to. They don't have an army, so you are their rulers. To keep control over them, and to make sure there isn't any trouble, tax them heavily and crush any of them that refuse to obey you."

"But what about the prince, we didn't kill the prince yet," replied one leader.

"We have time to find the prince. He is especially young, and when we do find him, he will be easy to deal with," replied the general. "Don't worry about the prince. I'll have our spies hidden in all the peasant villages. If the prince is out there, we will find him soon enough. In the meantime, you take care of running your villages and collecting lots of taxes."

"So when we find him, should I have him killed immediately?" asked the general's chief spy.

"No, first let's try and see if we can convince him to be one of us," replied the ever-thinking general. "Remember his father is dead. He is young and he won't remember much about his father," he sneered.

"Ah, so you want to make him one of us?" repeated the chief spy.

"Yes, if we can convert him into a chameleon prince, then he can be our little puppet King, all the appearance of a real King, but without any power. Yes, that would work very well for us. No rebel lizard would dare go against his true King. It would secure our hold on this land for a good long time," the general said with pleasure.

"As you wish, general," replied the chief spy. "I will report all to you as soon as we have located him."

"Very well, leave me now, I have a new castle to move into," the general responded with a neat little grin on his chameleon face.

CHAPTER 3

COMMON LIZARD
Seven years later

"Time for dinner kids."

Louie and his siblings came running from the yard. "What's for dinner tonight, Mom?" asked Louie.

"Just go wash your hands and you'll see," replied his mother.

Louie enjoyed summers in his home village with no school and lots of time to play outside with his friends. Louie was a strong lizard for his age. At ten-years-old, he was bigger than most of his friends. Good at sports and happy at home, Louie just wanted to make his parents proud, especially his dad. Louie had a very strong attachment to his father, even more so than his brother did. Louie was an unusual lizard in many ways. Because of his size, he tended to stick out of the crowd at school. This made him uncomfortable because he very much wanted to fit in. But for some reason, try as he would, Louie always felt different deep inside.

Although Louie tried to ignore it, he knew there were problems in his little village. The chameleons never seemed satisfied with their ever-increasing taxes. This caused the fathers in the village so much stress many of them were talking secretly of trying to overthrow the chameleons. However, the chameleons were masters at maintaining their control over the land. Their spies were skilled at identifying possible leaders that were a danger to their rule. Louie was too young to understand all this, but he felt the unrest in the air.

Most village lizards were kind and helpful towards children, but Louie had a strange feeling about the one that always hung out by the corner store. He was an odd-looking lizard and he was almost too nice. Louie wondered what he did for a living since he was at the same spot in the village every day. This strange lizard liked to draw anyone he could into conversation. At first Louie thought he was just an extra-friendly lizard. Then he thought, maybe this lizard was out of work and very lonely. But slowly Louie became convinced that there was something wrong about this lizard. Louie became even more uncomfortable as this village lizard started showing interest in him. It was as if the lizard knew Louie was different. Louie didn't like the feeling he got when the lizard was around, so he tried to avoid that corner store as much as he could.

"It's been seven years, you better be sure this time!" General Cramstack demanded. "Those blue bellies in the forest will die from old age before we'll ever let them have their prince!"

"We're sure we have the right one this time, sir," responded the chief spy.

"Did you check the birthmark?" Cramstack asked.

"Yes! The village spy, he's been suspicious for some time, finally got close enough and we are very sure," replied the chief spy.

"Excellent, excellent," said Cramstack. "Okay, what's the report on his living situation? How have they hid him so successfully all this time?"

The chief spy responded, "He has assumed the identity of a peasant lizard, as we came to suspect. He has a normal-looking family that he is a part of— a father, mother, one sister and one brother. He blends in very well, and our spies believe he doesn't know who he is. That is the reason, perhaps, that it took us so long to finally identify him."

"Interesting. This could be easier than I thought. Okay, now the fun part of our plan. First, I want your spies to stake out the village. Make sure no blue-belly warriors are around, I don't want them causing problems. Next, I want you to arrange for his happy little family to have some unfortunate accidents," Cramstack said, rubbing his hands together.

"Unfortunate accidents? What exactly do you want us to do?" asked the chief spy.

Cramstack began to pace. "Take out his peasant dad! Make it look like bad health or something. A ten-year-old without a dad, yes, that will make him defenseless to our powers. Next, after a small wait, take out his brother as well. We must remove all the important male role models from his world. Make that one look good also. You must not let him suspect we are behind these accidents. Then I want as much mistreatment as you can generate towards him. Find a way to cause his friends to abandon him. Make sure teachers are quick-tempered and mean towards him. Find some good bullies to make fun of him and, yes, get him into some fights at school. I want him as discouraged and weak as possible. Once we have successfully molded his world, so he feels all alone, we will make him ours!"

"This will take some time to organize and set in motion. How long do we have?" asked the chief spy.

"You have some time, but not too long. We have heard rumors that the blue-bellies are grabbing young male lizards at the age of fifteen to train in the forest somewhere. We absolutely cannot let Louie reach fifteen before we take him. So do what you must do, but complete the process before his fifteenth birthday and we will surprise those blue-bellies once again! Let me know when you are ready for the final weapon, and I'll send her in."

CHAPTER 4

ROUGH TIMES

Walking towards the corner store, Louie looked around wondering where that strange lizard had gone. When his mom asked him to fetch some groceries, Louie wanted to be helpful, but he wasn't eager to go back to that corner store. But much to his surprise, the nosy lizard was no-where to be found.

Glad to be away from the corner store, Louie walked home with the groceries his mother needed. Kicking rocks along the street, he kept himself occupied as he walked the many blocks back home. As he rounded the corner to his street, Louie noticed lots of lizards coming in and out of his house. *What's all this about?* he thought. Getting closer, he felt strangely sad. Then fear began to build within him, because the faces of the lizards showed concern and alarm. Louie knew something was very wrong.

"Dad is dead," his sister said as she looked past him with a stare.

What? She can't mean it, this can't be real, not my Dad, Louie thought. But the faces of his family and neighbors said it all. Tragedy had struck, suddenly and forcefully.

"But how?" Louie asked his mom. His mother was in shock and didn't seem to hear him. Louie quickly turned to his older brother, Porez.

"No one's really sure, Louie, but they think he had a bad heart or something. One moment he was eating lunch and the next he was...dead," Porez replied. "Now it's up to us, Louie, we have to be the leaders of the family. We have to help Mom out and we have to be strong, okay?"

Louie nodded, still not completely understanding or believing this was really happening.

The next few months were very strange for Louie. Neighbors and friends continually visited, bringing food and words of encouragement and support. But as time crept along, the visitors thinned out. Slowly, it became as if nothing had happened, except that his dad was gone, forever.

Louie ached. Not like the physical ache of an upset stomach, but an emotional ache, like someone had hit him in the gut and never pulled their fist back. Louie loved his dad. He loved to make his dad proud, to see him smile. But now there was nothing, just a big void.

Louie was thankful that at least he still had his brother. At least there was someone to talk to that understood. Louie spent many nights having long conversations with his brother. Their struggle brought them close.

After losing his father, Louie couldn't imagine things getting worse. But everything in his world began to change. Coming home from school, bullies started picking on him. Because he was large for his age, the bully types had always left Louie alone. But after his father died, the school bullies sensed a new weakness in him. And as these events increased, Louie finally told his brother about them. He didn't want to worry Porez, he had enough problems trying to be the head of the house, but Louie needed help.

"Tomorrow I'll come get you from school. We can take on those bullies together," Porez said firmly.

"Thanks," said Louie.

"We're brothers. We will get you through this," replied Porez.

Traveling with Porez, Louie felt confident and strong. His big brother was with him. *Those bullies won't try anything today,* he thought.

Rounding the corner, chills ran down Louie's spine. Something didn't feel right. In front of them were the three lizard bullies, waiting for them. Louie stopped.

"What's the matter," his brother asked.

"I'm not sure, but something doesn't feel right," Louie said, looking around.

"We can take these lizard bullies," replied Porez,

"don't worry."

Louie looked behind them. Sure enough two other large lizards were sneaking up behind them. They were very large for school-aged lizards.

Usually the bullies would taunt Louie, making fun of him, trying to bait him into a fight. This time they said nothing; they just rushed at them without a word.

"I think we better run," Louie said.

"We can't, Louie," Porez said with concern in his voice. "They've got us surrounded. We have to fight. I'll take the two large ones behind us, you take the three in front."

Louie and Porez fought well. They fought for each other. Using his tail as a whip, Porez was able to sting one of the large lizards as he hit the other. Meanwhile Louie lunged at one lizard knocking him backwards and then quickly jumped at another. Porez and Louie stuck close and kept moving to keep the lizards from hitting them from behind.

The brothers fought as best they could. Inspired to fight for each other, they held off the five attacking lizards very well. But suddenly they noticed five more coming from behind, with clubs.

Waking up in his own bed, Louie felt the lump on the back of his head. One good crack on the head and he was out. That's the last thing he remembered. He was amazed he had survived, and with only one really good lump. He felt lucky until he saw his sister's face. Then he knew. His brother hadn't been as lucky. He was dead.

Louie's whole life was crushed. First his dad, now his beloved brother. Louie just wanted to die. But he couldn't. His mother and sister were going to need him now more than ever. Louie was overcome with grief and the incredible stress of knowing he was now the head of the house. He would try and live on, but he knew his heart would never be the same.

The next few years for Louie were extremely hard. His family didn't have very much, now that his father wasn't there to provide. His friends at school kept away from him, like there was a curse on him and anyone who got too close to him. His teachers seemed especially mean to him, always expecting him to come up short, and so he usually did.

The bully attacks seemed to lessen. However, he was not unwilling to start a fight or two himself from time to time. Mad at what had happened to his family, mad at what had happened to him, Louie was one angry lizard. It seemed the whole world was against him and there was nothing he could do about it.

One day, as Louie was walking alone, he noticed some lizards coming his way. They looked like trouble. Louie was in no mood for that. He was exhausted from school and exhausted from life. As the lizards approached, Louie looked around. *There's got to be some way I can avoid them,* he thought. As he looked to his right, he saw a lizard poking his head through a slat in the fence.

"Come here," the lizard whispered. "This way!"

Louie was curious. What could this be? Another trap? Then he looked again at the lizards coming faster towards him. He made a quick decision and bolted for the fence.

As Louie approached, the fence slat opened slightly and Louie slipped inside.

"Shhhh," said the lizard behind the fence. "They didn't see where you went. So be quiet and stay here until I get them to leave. Give me one minute. I'll pop up on the other side, make them chase me, and then you'll be safe to go."

Not used to lizards being nice to him, Louie was confused. "Why are you doing this?" he asked.

"Because, you're the prince!" The lizard disappeared behind the other side of the fence.

Because, you're the prince? What? That lizard must think I'm someone else. Strange, Louie thought.

Louie peeked through a hole in the fence and

sure enough, the lizard who thought he was a prince popped up on the other side of the street. The friendly lizard made sure the pursuing lizards saw him and then he disappeared, running around the corner. The lizards outside the fence gave chase and were gone. Louie shrugged his shoulders, came out of hiding, and continued back home.

A prince. Hmmm. Me? Ha, that's funny, Louie thought, shaking his head.

"It's time, General," reported General Cramstack's chief spy.

"You sure?" replied the general.

"Yes. We've done all that you asked and now Louie is as weak as he is going to get. Moreover we're beginning to hear reports of blue-belly movements in his direction. We aren't completely sure, but we think they're targeting him very soon," answered the chief spy.

"Very well. Send her in," Cramstack said with a smile.

CHAPTER 5

TRINA

Louie knew many of the lizards his age were beginning to pair up with lizard friends of the opposite sex. But Louie preferred to be alone. The extra effort and possibility for embarrassment weren't attractive to him. When he was honest with himself, Louie admitted he was beginning to notice some of the prettier female lizards his age. He was passing into adulthood, and females had a strange attraction that often made him wish for the simpler days of childhood. Females were a confusing matter, and he didn't have any experience and no one to ask for advice. Some of the situations he had observed shocked him. As far as he could tell, many a poor male lizard was left humiliated and distressed by his unsuccessful attempts to obtain the friendship and affection of the pretty little female lizards. Others seemed successful, but their success seemed to change them so that hanging out with their male lizard friends was never enough anymore. All Louie knew was that he was more than willing to let the "experts" handle these matters. He was just trying to make it through his days one at a time.

After glancing his way several times, Trina was getting frustrated. Louie was completely unaware of her attempts to get his attention. "This is going to be harder than I thought," Trina said to herself.

Louie was in his own little world, and that world didn't include female lizards. But Trina was a determined lizard and Louie was a challenge.

Trina made sure that she was right in front of Louie as they left class that day. As they got outside, two of Trina's books slipped from her arms and fell at Louie's feet. Not paying attention, Louie tripped over them and fell face first on the floor. Trina chuckled. Embarrassed, Louie picked himself off the floor and bent down to get the books.

"Those are mine, thank you," Trina said, bending down next to Louie. As she took the books from Louie, she placed her hand on his for moment and tried to catch his eyes. Louie didn't seem to notice.

Extremely uncomfortable, he wanted to get out of this situation before he became anymore noticeable. "Yeah, sorry," Louie replied as he quickly made his escape.

Disappointed but not discouraged, Trina decided it was time to get bolder. Everywhere Louie went, Trina made sure she was there. Glancing, looking his way, and sometimes staring at him for moments at a time, Trina's charms slowly began to affect Louie. He couldn't ignore what was happening. He hadn't want-

ed to recognize her at all, but her determination was
wearing him down. It began with curiosity. Why
would a female lizard be so interested in him? He
began to return her glances. Then he found himself
getting caught by her eyes. Those eyes. They captured
him little-by-little with every look. Before Louie knew
what had happened, he was paired up with this
female lizard named Trina.

 Holding hands with her one day, he realized he
didn't know her very well at all. He wanted to ask her
questions and find out more about her, but she
always turned the conversation back to him. But as
he spent more time with her, he learned some things
about her by watching her carefully. Louie felt one of
the reasons Trina liked him so much was because he
was a large lizard. This made Louie very uncomfortable because inside Louie felt small. Trina liked
power. She liked the idea that Louie, being large,
could overpower other lizards if he wanted to. She
also felt powerful. He could tell she was very pleased
she had finally gotten Louie to notice and like her.
Louie wasn't sure if that made him feel wanted, or if it
made him feel like a trophy, or worse, like prey.

 As Louie wondered where this relationship with
Trina was going, Trina invited him to meet some of
her special friends. Louie was interested and curious.
He wanted to know more about her, so this was a

welcomed invitation.

"Meet me in this field tonight at midnight," she told him.

"At midnight?" he questioned.

"Just do what I say, you'll like it," she assured him.

That was one thing about Trina, she always knew her mind, knew what she wanted. She knew how to lead. And so, Louie would follow. He was too tied up in knots from all he had been through in his short life. Leading took energy and sure knowledge of what you wanted. Louie didn't have much of either. So he concluded that Trina was good for him. She made the decisions, and if she ordered him around a bit, that was okay. *Someone needs to lead*, he thought.

A little before midnight, Louie snuck out of his house and made his way to the field. Standing in the field, he waited. Minutes passed and Louie continued to wait. Finally, after half an hour, Louie assumed she wasn't coming and started to head home.

"Over here. Come over here," a voice called from the trees.

"Trina? Is that you?" Louie answered.

Louie heard nothing. But assuming it must be Trina, Louie walked towards the trees. Entering the tree line, two big reptiles grabbed Louie saying, "Ah yes, Louie, you will come with us."

"Who are you? Where's Trina?" Louie objected.

"You will see her soon enough. We will take you to her," they replied.

Louie felt strange, something wasn't right, but he was too tired to fight. He told himself Trina must have arranged this, so it would be all right.

Entering a large castle through the drawbridge, Louie became even more curious. They were taking him to an old castle? Trina was in the castle? Who were these friends of hers anyway? Louie was confused.

CHAPTER 6

CASTLE CLUES

The blue-belly scout burst into the blue-belly command meeting. "They've taken Louie! We can't find him anywhere! Sir, what are we going to do?"

"We underestimated[2] those chameleons again, I'm afraid," replied Talis. "But maybe this is all for the best."

"Excuse me sir, but how could Louie being taken by the chameleons be for the best? They'll brainwash him for sure. They must have known who he was for some time now. They could have just killed him. But since they didn't, it can only mean they want him alive, to be used for their own evil, dishonest purposes. Oh, commander, this is not good. We should attack now. Before it's too late!" replied the soldier.

"No. This could be very good. Louie may be open to their brainwashing, but, then again, he is the prince," Talis responded.

"But he was only three years old! How much could he possibly remember?" the soldier objected.

"We will do nothing for now," Talis commanded. "This is the perfect test. We all wanted to know what kind of king Louie would be. Now we will find out. If he falls under the control of the chameleons...then he never would have made it as king anyway. But, if he

---

[2] underestimate - to think less than what they are

has the strength of character his father had, if the royal blood flowing through his veins is strong enough, then he *will* make it through. So for now, we do nothing. We will watch and wait...and hope."

Going through the dark castle corridors, Louie could hardly see. But something seemed strangely familiar, as if he had been here before. *Silliness,* he thought. But something kept coming back to him. The smell, the smell was familiar. Maybe his family had lived someplace with similar smells when he was younger. He didn't really remember his early child-hood, and his family never spoke of it. So this was very possible.

Suddenly they entered a room with bright torchlights all around. Louie shielded his eyes. It was no use. He couldn't see anything.

"Welcome, young Louie," a gruff voice spoke from behind the lights. "We are the chameleon ruler-ship, and we have heard that you want to join us."

"I do?" Louie muttered.

"Yes, I am the princess and you can be my prince!"

"Trina? Is that you?" Louie asked.

"First we must see if he is the right material to be one of us. We must see if he has the strength and smarts to be of the ruling class, to be a royal

chameleon," the other voice said again. "We will teach
you each night and test you each morning. If you
pass, you become one of us. If you don't, well, let's
just say that your mother and sister are hoping you
pass."

Louie's stomach sank. *Who are these lizards?*
I'm sure that one voice is Trina. But who are her
friends? Where has she taken me? And why are they
threatening my family?

That night the educating began.

"Chameleons are the best," began the gruff
voice behind the bright lights. "Chameleons fought
the blue-belly lizard army and defeated them because
the blue-belly king was evil."

"Why was he evil? What did he do?" Louie
asked.

There was no answer. After a long moment of
silence, the chameleon with the gruff voice and those
with him walked out and shut the door. Louie was left
alone in his dark, locked room.

Two nights later, the chameleons returned.

"Chameleons are the best," the gruff voice said
again. "Chameleons fought the blue-belly lizard army
and defeated them because the blue-belly king was
evil."

"Why was he..." Louie's voice trailed off as he

rubbed his stomach. Tired and hungry, he gave in to the silent pressure.

Taking a deep breadth, Louie said slowly, "Chameleons defeated the evil blue-belly king and his army because chameleons are the best."

Night after night, he couldn't tell how many, he was told about the history of how the chameleons became rulers of the land. Of how the chameleons had overcome the evil blue-bellies and their wicked king. How chameleons were better reptiles than any other lizard and therefore it was their right to rule. Then every morning he was tested about every detail and story from the night before. If he answered well, he ate well. If he didn't, then he didn't eat at all. Louie learned fast. He learned to say what they wanted to hear and to say it like he believed it. After a while, Louie wasn't sure what he believed and what he didn't. But for now, he didn't care, as long as he got to eat. Or so he told himself.

After some time the test was over. He felt like he had graduated. For the first time he got to see the face behind the gruff voice. His name was General Cramstack. He said the old king, who was murdered by blue-bellies, had put him in charge. He was supposed to protect the princess and find her a worthy prince. Then the two would rule, with his guidance and protection, of course. No one came out and said it, but Louie realized that he was being groomed to be that prince. Louie wondered why he was chosen from all the lizards in the land. But by now he knew better than to ask, so he just continued acting as expected. He thought about asking Trina, but she had become very distant and cold since coming to the castle. Louie didn't want to be *their* prince. He was homesick and really wanted to run away. But he told himself cooperating would help his mother and sister the most, so he did.

Walking through the castle, Louie doubted the two chameleon guards following him were really assigned for his protection, as he was told. It reminded him of that nosy lizard back in his home village— same feeling.

As he passed the library, something inside caught his curiosity—books. He felt drawn to go inside. The guards were a little concerned and confused. They whispered to each other as if they weren't sure whether Louie was allowed to be in the library. Louie ignored them. He sensed that somewhere in these books there might be some answers to his many questions. He went to a bookshelf and scanned the titles. A gentle familiar feeling came over him.

It's as if I've been here before, he thought. Louie

took a deep breath and closed his eyes, hoping to bring back the memory of something long forgotten. Louie reached to take a book from the shelf. This was too much for the guards.

Rushing towards Louie one of them said, "You need to go now, the general wants to see you."

"Yeah, Trina wants to see you, umm, I mean the general wants to see you," said the other.

As they were grabbing him by the arms to take him outside, Louie noticed a folded piece of paper in the bookshelf where he had taken the book. A desperate feeling came over him; he had to have that paper. He quickly tossed his book to the floor.

"Whoops," he said. As the guards turned their heads towards the floor, Louie freed one of his arms, quickly snatched the paper, and hid it beneath his scales.

As they carried him out, Louie burned with curiosity and frustration. He was growing very tired of feeling so used and not knowing why. If he was really going to be the prince, then why did he have so little freedom? Louie wanted answers.

Louie knew he was being watched. The only time the two guards weren't hovering over him was when he was in a room with Trina. This early evening he was glad to have the opportunity to face Trina alone. This was his chance to get some answers.

Trina was in a very bad mood this day, so Louie was-n't sure how to start. But with frustration mounting deep within, Louie simply said, "I'm not sure I want to be a prince!"

"What!" Trina snapped. Then almost as quickly, she softened. "Why do you say that Louie?" she asked sweetly.

Louie, a little shocked at the quick change in mood, continued. "I feel like a prisoner here. Those two gorillas follow me everywhere I go. If this is the life of a prince, then I'm not interested!" Louie said with growing boldness.

"Tomorrow we will go out into some villages and you can see what it's like to rule your subjects. That should be fun. Let me go get the general. He can tell you more about what he has planned for tomorrow." Trina quickly left the room.

It took a few moments, but suddenly Louie remembered the paper, and that he was alone. He quickly took it out, unfolded it and looked. It was a drawing of a strong and noble-looking lizard with a crown on his head. He noticed the blue belly, the large sword and the face. Those eyes, that face. Louie peered deeper into the picture. Why did this face look so familiar, so warm? This didn't look like the evil blue-belly king he had imagined when the chameleons told him their story. But there it was, a crown on his head. This had to be the blue-belly king he was told about. But those eyes...Louie looked long at the face. Why did he feel so warm inside looking into this lizard's face? *Maybe there's more to this story than the chameleons have told me,* he thought. Hearing footsteps, Louie put the picture away.

"Tomorrow we will go into the villages and I'll teach you how to rule," the general stated blandly as he burst into the room with Trina on his heels.

"Now don't leave him alone in here again," he whispered firmly to Trina.

And with that the general disappeared again. Trina seemed nervous and upset. Louie decided it was best to play along so he might get more chances to gather information and clues. "Okay. Tomorrow sounds like it might be fun," he said. Louie left Trina, and as soon as he was in the hallway his two escorts quickly found him, and took him to his room.

CHAPTER 7

CHAMELEON POWER

The next day, Louie found himself on a royal carriage. Seated next to Trina, he looked around to see their entire guard. Chameleon soldiers with spears all around, and at the head, the general with his sword. As they approached the village, most peasants ran into their homes, while three brave male lizards stood their ground to face them.

"Make way, make way," the chameleon guards called out.

As they came to a stop in the village square, the three village lizards stepped up to General Cramstack. "What is your business here?" they asked firmly.

"Your village is behind in their taxes. If you will not pay, we will make an example out of your village today," the general said, staring down at the village lizards with his chest puffed out. General Cramstack loved to bully the peasant lizards. He enjoyed the feeling of power it gave him. But to his disappointment these lizards showed no fear.

"I said, we will make an example of your village if you don't pay up!" he said loudly.

One of the lizards motioned with his head signaling the village lizards. "How much do you say we owe this time?" one of the lizards asked.

Cramstack, having noticed the subtle[3] signal,

---

[3] subtle – gently done in the hope no one will see

looked around. "Where are the rest of the village lizards? What was that signal you just made?" He paused for a second, and when he didn't get an immediate answer, he motioned for his guards to start searching the huts. Prompted by the signal, village lizards were escaping into the forest from behind their homes. Once the guards realized what was happening, they started grabbing any peasant lizards they could catch. Screaming and running, the peasant lizards ran, hid, and climbed trees to escape. There were too many lizards and not enough guards, so most of the lizards got away. But the ones that were caught, were brought into the square and thrown down next to the three male lizards still holding their ground in front of Cramstack.

One soldier grabbed a young female lizard and, as she struggled, threw her against Louie's carriage. Louie looked over at the young lizard. For a moment their eyes met. Louie could see the pain and the struggle in her eyes. He looked more deeply. She reached out towards him and with her eyes asked him for help.

Trina's scepter came down hard. Smack! "Get this peasant trash away from my carriage," she snapped. The chameleon guards quickly pulled her away from the carriage and threw her down with the rest of the captured lizards.

"Marie, are you all right?" one of the male lizards whispered to his captured daughter.

"Yeah. Just a little scared. But Mom and the kids made it," Marie whispered back.

"Okay. On my signal you make a run for it. Got it?" Marie's father directed.

"Dad, no. What are you going to do? No, Dad..." Marie pleaded.

"I love you Marie. Tell Mom and the kids how much I love them. And tell them to be brave and I'll see them on the other side." With that, he leapt up and grabbed Cramstack's sword, catching him by surprise. The two lizards wrestled on the ground. Marie paused, but understanding that there was nothing left to do, she ran.

With all eyes focused on the struggling lizards, no one noticed Marie until too late. She made it into the forest and hid behind a rock. Peering from behind her cover, Marie watched as the guards grabbed her father from behind. Cramstack regained his feet and drew his sword. She winced as she saw the sword flash. It was over quickly. Her dad had died well. With bravery and courage he gave his life to save hers. She would never forget.

Tears welling in her eyes, with both sadness and pride, she whispered, "Goodbye daddy. I'll see you on the other side." Then she quickly turned, running into the forest in the hope of finding what was left of her family.

Louie was glad to see her escape. He couldn't get the picture of her looking up at him out of his mind. *And what did he see in her eyes?* He thought. *Strength, yes, and courage...and yet, also a softness, all at the same time.* Could deep compassion and strong belief really be alive in someone so easily, so smoothly? Then it dawned on him. He had seen this somewhere before. But where? Ah yes, the picture of that blue-belly king. He had the same look.

Louie felt strange. Like these peasant lizards had something he didn't have. But he was the one with power. They were mere peasants. One of them just paid with his life. But what was this strange attraction and respect he felt? As if someone were calling him to leave all he had, and join them in their struggle. *Nonsense*, he thought. He chuckled.

"What's so funny?" Trina demanded, hearing him chuckle.

"Nothing," Louie responded, knowing he could never share these thoughts with Trina.

"All you lizards have committed crimes and therefore you will be made examples for all the peasant lizards to learn from! Refusing to pay the commanded taxes, helping in the escape of runaway lizards, and attacking a royal chameleon, for all these crimes you will all die!" Cramstack pronounced.

A few of the younger captured lizards whimpered. "Be brave children," the older male lizard whispered.

"Take them to the open field," Cramstack commanded.

The general moved over and whispered something to the two guards assigned to Louie. Then the whole group of chameleon guards, the carriage and captured lizards moved out into the open field. It didn't take long for the birds to appear. In the open field the lizards were helpless. Quickly Cramstack commanded all chameleons to change color. "Blend now!" he shouted. Each chameleon became part of the background.

"How do I blend? I'm not a chameleon, am I?" Louie asked.

"Just close your eyes and picture the color you want to be," Trina said softly. "Hurry up, close your eyes."

The two guards next to Louie very carefully spread a camouflage[4] blanket above him so he didn't feel it.

"That's it. You've got to keep your eyes closed though. Wait until the general gives the command and then you can open them, but not until then,"

---

[4] camouflage – to hide or conceal by means of disguise

Trina told him.

Sure enough, the chameleons and Louie were invisible to the birds, but the peasant lizards were not. In a few quick moments the birds were done. With the last of the birds flying off, Cramstack gave the command to return.

"You can open your eyes now," said Trina.

Looking around, Louie couldn't believe his eyes. Blood stains and lizard parts were everywhere. It was not a pretty sight. Louie felt sick. *This is the general's lesson in how to rule? What kind of chameleons are they?* Louie thought with disgust.

"You changed colors very well," Trina said with a twinkle in her eye.

"What?" Louie said, still getting over the shock of the massacre.

"You changed colors very well. You are a fine chameleon," Trina continued.

"I am? I'm a chameleon? Are you sure?" Louie said skeptically.

"You changed colors didn't you?" Trina answered.

She has a point, Louie thought. *Otherwise the birds would have picked me off.*

"Yeah, guess I am a pretty decent chameleon," Louie said, not sure if being a chameleon was such a good thing.

Riding in the royal carriage was very comfortable. Louie tried not to think of the lizard massacre as they started back through the woods towards the castle. All of a sudden there was a flash of steel and war cries! Louie sat up, and to his amazement, he saw blue-belly lizards attacking the chameleon guards. They came quickly and caught the general and his soldiers by surprise. Trina screamed. Several blue-bellies were engaging the general with their swords. Cramstack was backing up, trying to hold the blue-bellies off, and before Louie knew what was happening, the carriage toppled over.

"Retreat! Retreat!" Cramstack yelled. "Make for the castle, hurry!"

Louie had fallen out over the side of the road and tumbled into a pile of leaves. He heard the clash of steel and the general's command, but he wasn't sure what to do. In an instant, he made up his mind. Louie ran and he ran fast...*away* from the castle. He ran and ran and ran. He didn't stop running even after the sound of clashing steel faded into the distance.

CHAPTER 8

FOREST DREAM

Exhausted and lost, Louie ran into a hedge of bushes to hide. But inside the hedge was a young bird that saw him. The bird had been feeding on bugs all day, but quickly moved to capture Louie. Seeing the bird coming, Louie thought, *Ah, I will just stand still and change my color so that I blend into the background. The bird will never see me, and I will be safe.* As he stood perfectly still, the bird came up from behind him and grabbed him by his tail and flew to the top of the bush.

Louie was shocked. *How did it see me?* he thought as he dangled upside down from the bird's mouth. *I camouflaged myself; I'm a chameleon! Chameleons are not supposed to be caught so easily!*

The young bird was full from eating bugs, so after admiring it's catch, it let him go free beside a tree. Louie quickly scampered up the tree and breathed a huge sigh of relief. Wondering what went wrong with his chameleon camouflage, he rested for a while and waited for his pounding heart to calm down.

Suddenly the sound of something big in the tree startled him. A snake! Looking to eat him! Louie ran around the backside of the tree and again decided to blend into the background. But this time he kept a clear eye on the snake, just in case. Sure enough the camouflage did not work! The snake came right at Louie and he was forced to run. The snake narrowly missed him several times before he made it into some nearby bushes.

Louie was very frustrated. "How come my cam-ouflage isn't working? This could get me killed," he said out loud.

"He thinks he's a chameleon!" came a voice.

"Ha ha, that's really funny!" came another voice.

Surprised, Louie looked around. About twenty yards behind him were two blue-belly lizards pointing their little fingers at him and laughing. Louie climbed out of the bushes and as he approached them their laughter just increased.

Holding their blue-bellies from laughing so hard, they rolled on the dirt for quite some time. As they rolled around they said, "You ain't no chameleon! If you're a chameleon, I'm a komodo dragon, ha, ha!"

Still confused from his failed camouflage attempts, Louie was devastated[5]. Trina told him he was a chameleon and a part of him liked the idea that he could avoid danger by changing color. Could it be that he really didn't have camouflage abilities after all? But what about the camouflage in the field when the birds attacked? How could this be? Louie was

---

[5] devastated – shocked and helpless, completely discouraged

tired of being so confused and not knowing who he was. He became angry. Louie walked over to one of the laughing lizards and grabbed him by the throat. Lifting him off the ground, he demanded, "Then what am I, smart stuff?"

The laugher stopped. The suspended lizard looked him right in the eye and said, "You are the prince!"

With these words Louie woke up. After escaping from the chameleon carriage, Louie had run deep into the forest. Exhausted, he had fallen asleep deep inside some bushes.

Wow, what a strange dream, Louie thought, as he climbed out of the bushes. He looked around, not knowing where to go next. Faintly in the distance Louie heard voices. Without thinking, he walked in the direction of the voices.

After walking a short distance, Louie came upon the peasant lizards that had escaped from the village earlier. He was glad not to be alone in these dangerous woods. However, he wasn't sure how these lizards would treat him. He walked, slowly passing several gathered lizards, but they simply nodded to him without much concern. He took up a seat beneath a tree and watched them for a while. They took little interest in him so he slowly became more comfortable. He noticed they had what seemed like a village within the woods. Lizards were coming and going, but he didn't see any huts anywhere. He concluded that this must be some sort of lizard meeting place. He felt safer among these lizards than in the woods so he stuck around. As he rested under the tree, Louie's mind spun.

Moments later, he looked up and saw a familiar face staring down at him.

"What are you doing here?" asked the young female lizard. "You're that prince, aren't you! I saw you at the village, you were with the chameleons!"

Shaken back to reality, Louie remembered. He remembered that he was with the chameleons as they destroyed this poor lizard's village. This was the lizard that was thrown up against his carriage, who plead for help with her eyes, the one with strength in her, the one who had narrowly escaped. Louie rose to his feet wanting to quiet her down.

"I...I was...I am, I'm sorry," he said. "I'm so sorry." Louie hung his head and didn't know what else to say.

She paused and looked him over. Looking into his eyes, she realized he was not so dangerous after all. She softened. "My name is Marie," she said, extending her hand.

"Louie, my name is Louie," he said taking her hand and shaking it softly.

After an uncomfortable silence, Marie said, "I should take you to meet the commander. He would definitely like to meet you. Come on, follow me."

CHAPTER 9

NEW BEGINNING

"We don't know where he went. We attacked and the next time we looked, he was gone!" the soldier complained.

"Now what are we going to do?" questioned another soldier.

"Hold on, all is not lost. We just have to think this thing through," said commander Talis.

"Excuse me, sir." All heads turned as Marie spoke. "I have someone here that I know you will all want to meet," she said, as Louie entered the command tent behind her.

"Oh my!" said one.

"Well, would you believe it!" said another.

"Is that really him?" questioned another.

Talis slowly walked over to Louie and said, "Welcome good prince. I am Talis, the commander of the blue-belly forces. It is very good to see you here."

Louie was overwhelmed[6]. Talis and the blue-belly lizards had insisted that before any serious explanations occurred, he was to be fed and given time to rest. Now he was lying in a comfortable peasant bed and a meeting was scheduled for tomorrow morning with the commander.

---

[6] overwhelmed – overloaded, overcome and upset

As he lay on his bed, his mind kept returning to the same question: who was he really? He always thought growing up that he was an ordinary lizard. Then Trina and the chameleons had convinced him he was a very powerful chameleon prince. And then there was that dream he had, laughing lizards saying he was not a chameleon, but a prince? Louie knew it was just a dream, but deep down he hoped it was true.

Louie felt confused and a little excited, all at the same time. Something told him tomorrow's meeting with Talis would help him get some answers. And why did Talis call him "good prince?"

Looking at his situation, one thing was becoming very clear to Louie. He liked these blue-belly lizards much better than the chameleons. With the chameleons everything was about power, and he constantly felt like a thing to be used. On the other hand, these blue-bellies showed him kindness and respect. As far as they knew, especially Marie, he *was* a chameleon. And he was the chameleon prince sitting over the village massacre, yet they treated him well. Maybe he was their prisoner. He didn't really know. But he didn't mind. *This surely feels better than being with those grumpy old chameleons*, he thought as he drifted off to sleep.

As all the blue-belly leaders were entering the room, Talis was in deep thought. Once all the leaders were seated, Talis began.

"Now you all know that we have Louie, the son of our beloved King, here with us in camp. We have two immediate issues. First, as soon as the chameleons gather themselves and realize we have Louie, they will seek revenge on his family. So I need volunteers to fetch his mother and sister from their peasant village right away. Secondly, I need you all to help me with Louie. I'm pretty sure he doesn't know who he is. If we just walk up and tell him, it will be too much. I want to bring him to this realization slowly, but I need your help. As long as it takes, I need you all to treat him just like an ordinary lizard. He has been with the chameleons for a while, so I need time to prepare him."

"How will we know when he's ready?" asked one of the leaders.

"I'll know, we will all know when he's ready," Talis responded.

"You pointed out that he has been with those dirty chameleons for some time. So how do we know if he will *ever* be ready?" asked another.

"We don't," replied Talis somberly. "But we must be hopeful and give him the chance to become all that his father was, and maybe more. Remember, his father didn't become a great king overnight either. He had his struggles. I was there. I know. Now it's Louie's turn. All we can do is be there and help him when we can. But the decisions of the heart will be his to make, as it is with all of us."

With that, Talis chose the volunteers to rescue Louie's family. Hoping they were not too late, the lizards went off into the forest and toward Louie's old village. Meanwhile Talis continued in deep thought, trying to grab hold of the wisdom to help Louie find his answers.

The next morning Talis wakened Louie, "Time to get up, my good prince, we have work to do."

Louie was surprised to notice it was still dark. *Well, I guess being a prince isn't so easy with these blue-bellies,* he thought. But being curious and anxious for answers, Louie did what he was told and followed Talis into the forest.

"Just to let you know, we brought your mother and sister here to our village. We were able to get them late last night, and not a moment too soon from the report I've heard," Talis told him.

"Thank you," replied Louie. Louie hadn't seen his family since the chameleons took him into the castle months ago. He was looking forward to seeing them again. But this just brought up all the questions. What would he tell them? That he was a chameleon prince, and then he had run away from the chameleons to join the blue-belly army? Or that he ran away and became a prisoner of the blue-bellies? Louie's confusion must have shown all over his face.

"Are you all right?" asked Talis.

"Yes. I mean no, no," replied Louie. "Am I your prisoner?"

Talis laughed. "Why no, good prince, you are not my prisoner."

Louie's eyes thinned, "Why do you call me 'good prince'?"

"Because you are a prince, and I want you to be a good one," Talis responded.

Louie was still confused. "So am I a chameleon? Or am I a blue-belly like you?"

Talis smiled. "Which do you want to be?"

Louie didn't like this answer coming back as a question. But it was a good question. Honestly Louie was too tired to choose. He just wanted someone to tell him who he was, and then he could just accept it and go on. Louie sighed, "I don't know."

"Well, take some time to think it over. In the meantime, let's get working," Talis said, as he handed Louie a sword and shield.

"What's this?" Louie asked very surprised.

"It's my job to teach you how to be a prince, a good prince. And all princes must know how to fight!" Talis answered. And with that, Talis began teaching Louie how to fight. He took many days and taught him how to handle a sword and a shield. He taught him battle tactics and strategy. And in between the physical lessons, Talis taught Louie wisdom in how to rule the lizards with fairness and mercy. Talis was teaching Louie how to be like his father.

CHAPTER 10

ANGRY CHAMELEONS

General Cramstack was in a rage. Chameleons cowered all over the room. The general could not contain himself. "Lost, lost? How could you bumbling idiots lose the prince? If he makes contact with those blue-bellies in the forest our plan is finished! Ouch!" Trina was putting a bandage on his wounded arm.

"But he doesn't know who he is," Trina said calmly.

"Are you sure his belly hasn't turned blue?" Cramstack asked nervously.

"Of course not. We have him convinced he's a chameleon," she said confidently. "We got to him before he became an adult blue-belly, which means the power of our lies has him fully contained. As long as he remains a nice quiet, cowardly lizard, his chest will never turn blue. So, no matter what they tell him, he'll look in the mirror and there just won't be any blue on his belly! Even if he's with those blue-bellies right now, they can *never* convince him of his true identity."

"Good!" Cramstack said, somewhat relieved. "Where is my chief spy?" Cramstack yelled.

"Here I am, sir," he replied, walking into the room.

"Well, it's about time. I need to know where the

blue-bellies are hiding. What are your spies telling you?" Cramstack demanded.

"We are making great progress sir. However, we haven't determined their exact location as of yet," the chief replied, bowing his head. "But you will be glad to hear that our spies are in place throughout the peasant villages. Even if the blue-bellies try to fight, most peasants will be unwilling to join them. We have them convinced that we chameleons are too strong for them. They have no leaders, and without leaders they cannot fight us."

"So the answer is no, eh? Well you better get moving. The longer it takes the bigger the chance the prince will figure out who he really is. And if that happens, he will have to die. And it would be very sad if Trina lost her prince, now wouldn't it?" sneered Cramstack.

Looking down at her claws without concern, Trina asked calmly, "You would have him killed?"

"Yep!" Cramstack replied. "But don't you worry, we'll just find you a new prince." He smiled.

"A new one?" Trina said with hopeful curiosity.

"One that's much stronger and one that understands the ways of using power, unlike that weakling Louie," Cramstack said with disgust.

"Hmmm." Trina smiled, thinking of the possibilities.

Turning his attention back to his chief spy, Cramstack commanded, "Now report back to me as soon as you determine the location of the blue-belly camp. And hurry."

"Yes sir, general!" the chief spy replied. He saluted and left the room.

CHAPTER 11

WHO AM I?

Sitting beneath a tree to get out of the noonday sun, Louie was both exhausted and excited. The daily physical workouts with Talis were tough but enjoyable. Louie was a large lizard and he could tell his skill was increasing with every lesson. He loved the physical exercise with a purpose. Louie put his heart into every lesson and Talis seemed impressed with his progress.

Each day, in between the morning exercises and the afternoon strategy sessions, Marie would bring Talis and Louie lunch. Every time Louie saw Marie, he remembered the village massacre and felt very guilty. But Marie never showed any bitterness towards him, even though Louie knew she had lost many friends that day, maybe even family members. Usually she would bring the lunch and speak with Talis, then she would leave them again. But today Talis had some business and so he left Louie with Marie for a while.

"Do you mind if I sit?" Marie asked.

"No, go ahead," Louie replied.

"So, how's the training going?" Marie queried.

"Good. Talis is a great teacher," Louie answered.

"I need to ask you about that day in the village," Marie started. "I need to know some things, and

I just can't wait any longer to ask you." Louie's eyes got big and his heart started to pound. Marie continued, "Were you in charge that day?"

"In charge? What do you mean?" Louie felt very small.

"Could you have stopped the massacre? Could you have saved..." Marie started to lose it, tears welling up in her eyes. She paused, wiped her eyes forcefully and said, "I need to know if you were in charge. Are you the chameleon prince and were those your troops?" she demanded.

Louie shook his head slowly. "I am not sure *who* I am," he said. Painfully, Louie tried to think through the events of that day. "Those were not my troops, I don't think I could have stopped them even if I wanted to. General Cramstack...he is always in control," Louie paused again. "But I should have tried, I should have tried to stop them. I was just too afraid," Louie said as he dropped his head.

Marie was losing the fight to hold back her tears. She looked away. "Very well, I believe you." She started to get up.

"Please don't go," Louie said quickly. "I need to...I would like to talk to you more, if that's alright with you."

"Okay just give me a minute," she said still looking away and wiping her eyes. Finally after a long minute, she turned back toward Louie and nodded.

"I need to ask you, why did you look at me the way you did when you were thrown up against my carriage?" Louie asked softly.

"Because I thought you were in charge, you were the chameleon prince, you and your bride-to-be, princess or whatever. You were up there and it looked like you had the authority to stop what I knew was going to be a massacre," Marie answered. "So I was asking you to help, to help me and my family."

"And I let you down," Louie said, lowering his head again.

"You didn't have any authority, not really. I should have known it was hopeless, but I was hop-ing," Marie stopped.

Standing up, Louie pounded his fist into his palm and said, "Ahhh grumph! I should have done something! I was a wimp! I knew you were asking me for help. I could see it in your eyes. But I did nothing! I let Cramstack have his massacre. Many lizards lost their lives and families, because I did nothing!" Louie stared out into the distance as anger and grief caused tears of determination to well up in his eyes.

Marie stood silently looking at Louie, watching something come over him, which she had seen some-where before. "Louie, do you know who I lost that day?" she asked softly.

"No, no I don't," Louie said, afraid to hear the answer.

"I lost my dad." Marie began to cry. Gathering herself she continued, "Do you remember how I got away?"

"Yeah, that older lizard attacked Cramstack," Louie smiled. "He sure didn't expect that! And then you...oh," Louie paused. "I see. That was your dad, wasn't it?"

"Yes," Marie strained to hold back more tears. Looking away she whispered, "That was my daddy."

"Brave lizard," Louie said with admiration[7].

After a few moments, Marie gathered herself, spun around and looked Louie in the face. "And you have his courage!" Marie said firmly.

"What?" Louie blurted out.

"Yes, I have heard it said many times, that when someone dies, the spirit in which they die gets passed on to those that are willing to accept it. I can tell by the look on you, right now, that you have caught the spirit of courage that my dad died with!" Marie stood facing Louie with teary eyes and her jaw tightening. "Go with it Louie, take it as your own, and then you will know who you are." And with that, Marie got up and left.

Louie stared in shock as she walked away. A flood of emotion stirred inside him. How could Marie

---

[7] admire –to esteem highly, to look up to

be so encouraging, so kind, so inspiring towards him when he was partly responsible for the death of her father? But Louie couldn't deny it, he felt different. He felt bigger, stronger...and unafraid.

CHAPTER 12

IT FALLS TO ME

As Talis returned, he noticed something different about Louie. There was a deeper thoughtfulness about him. Talis saw an increase in maturity. "Did you have a good talk with Marie?" he asked.

"Yeah," Louie replied.

"What did you talk about?" Talis asked.

"Hard stuff," Louie answered.

"Good. Good," Talis replied. *Maybe it is time*, Talis thought.

"Louie?" Talis started.

"Yes," Louie looked over at him for the first time in their conversation.

"Have you decided what you want to be, or more accurately, *who* you want to be?" Talis asked him.

"I know I don't want to be a chameleon, that's for sure!" Louie paused and thought some more. "I'm really confused, Talis; I'm feeling so many things right now. But I don't understand your question. I mean, I am what I am, right? But the chameleons, they're cruel and without mercy. They are the rulers, but they treat the peasants like dirt. And that General Cramstack, I really don't like him at all. You've been so good to me, teaching me all this great stuff, trying to make me a good prince, but I really don't want to be a prince, not for those chameleons."

"Well said, good prince, well said," Talis said with a smile.

"And Talis, no offense, but please don't call me 'good prince' anymore. I'm not a good prince. I don't know if Marie told you, but I was at the village when the massacre happened. I was the 'chameleon prince', and I did nothing to stop it. Marie lost her father, and I did nothing," Louie said with self-disgust.

Talis waited to catch Louie's eyes. "I call you 'good prince' because I know who you are Louie. I know who you are." Looking away and towards the distant sky, Talis said under his breath, "And I knew your father."

"What did you say?" Louie asked.

Talis spun around and looked Louie square in the eyes and said, "It's time for me to tell you. Louie, you *are* a prince. But not a chameleon prince, you are the son of the blue-belly king. You are, and always have been, the next king of the blue-bellies. Your father was my king and my best friend. I served him; I was his commander. And I left him that day, that day the chameleons tricked us, attacked and over-came us. But I only left him because he commanded me to. Because of you. Because I was supposed to save you from the chameleons."

"What?" Louie was stunned. "You mean I really

am a blue-belly lizard, not a chameleon after all? But then...how come my belly is not blue?"

"The color of your belly is not what makes you a blue-belly, Louie. It's your heart. I can't really answer why your belly isn't blue. It should have turned blue a long time ago. Maybe it's some form of chameleon curse, I don't know. But what I do know, is that you are the son of the great blue-belly king. And maybe when you finally step into your destiny, as his son, then that curse will be broken."

Louie remembered the picture in his scales. Pulling it out, he began unfolding it, still half-stunned. "And this picture," Louie said softly, "is a picture of my real dad?"

Looking over Louie's shoulder, Talis was amazed and glad to see the face of his beloved king again. "Yes! Yes Louie, that's your real dad, King Scelo, my old friend."

In a flash, Talis remembered all the battles they had fought together, the victories, the defeats, the companionship, and the deep bond he had had with his old friend and king. And then he remembered his friend's last request, "Tell my son I love him." He remembered the last time he saw his face, as if it were yesterday.

"Louie," Talis started. "King Scelo, your father, told me to tell you something that day. I've been waiting twelve years to tell you. The last thing he told me, before I left him, before he died, was to tell you...that he loved you," Talis said as he started to choke up.

"Really?" Louie asked softly. A flood of warmth slowly overcame him. As Louie dwelt on those words, and all they meant to him, he felt strength entering his soul. Could it be, after so many years of being so lost and confused, he was finally grasping who he really was?

Talis went on to explain how Louie was the pride and joy of his father. He told him about living in the castle, and the great promise that Louie repre-sented, for all the blue-belly lizards in his father's kingdom. He then told Louie of that fateful day, when through lies and trickery, the chameleons killed his father, and took the land. And how Louie was hidden in a peasant family, until it was time for him to be king.

This new identity was going to take a while before it felt comfortable, but Louie liked the good news. He was *not* a chameleon. He was the son of a great blue-belly king! Louie liked this new way of see-ing himself. He felt a new freedom, a whole new beginning to his life.

"What was he like Talis? Tell me about him," Louie begged.

"Oh, he was brave, and strong, and good," Talis

began.

Talis and Louie talked for hours. Talis enjoyed telling Louie as many stories as he could remember. It was like bringing the old king back to life. And as Talis told the stories, he realized how much he had missed his old friend.

Talis told Louie about some of the greatest battlefield victories. How his father, the king, had outsmarted his enemies with superior strategy and tactics. How the blue-belly troops were always the best prepared and the best trained. "But," Talis said with a twinkle in his eye, "the most powerful gift your father had, was his ability to inspire us. Even when we were outnumbered, your father motivated[8] us with the highest values. He reminded us of the reasons we must fight, and then he led us to amazing victory after amazing victory." Talis went on to tell Louie how the land was safe under the king's leadership for many years.

"So how did it all end this way?" Louie asked with concern.

"A new kind of weapon, Louie. A new kind of weapon," Talis said, shaking his head.

"You tell me how brave, strong and noble my father was. What new weapon defeated him? I have to know," Louie insisted.

"You've seen it. You already know what it is,"

---

[8] motivate – rally, inspire, excite, stir

Talis replied.

"Lies and deception? Simple deception has that much power?" Louie asked doubtfully.

"Not just simple deception, *chameleon* deception. The kind of deception that had you believing you were a chameleon. The kind of deception that seems so real, that seems so rooted in truth, that most believe it. It's hard to explain, but the deception plays to its victim's weaknesses. It has a power all it's own. It can separate the best of friends, and it can fool the smartest of lizards. Komo, the monitor lizard, believed it. And that's the only reason the chameleons defeated your father that day," Talis explained.

"Wow. So how do you defeat it?" Louie asked.

"You believe. You must believe past the lies. Believe the truth despite what your eyes tell you. Then you must expose the lies, and expose the real truth, and that's not easy. Look, what your father did was defeat the enemies of his day. He made great progress. He was truly a great king," Talis paused. "But he also used to tell me, 'Every generation will have it's own battles to fight.' You know, I never really understood that. He really started saying that to me after you were born. I think he realized that his abilities were only going to take us so far. I think he knew there were things he wouldn't be able to do, things that would fall to you, the next generation."

"Interesting," Louie marveled[9]. "And so it falls to me...and so it falls to me," Louie slowly repeated.

---

[9] marvel - to become filled with surprise, wonder; amazed curiosity

CHAPTER 13

DESTINY

As Louie and Talis continued to talk, darkness began to fall. Suddenly, something rushed towards them from behind. Swoosh. It was over in an instant. Talis was standing over the dead body of a chameleon. Louie barely had time to get up. "What was that?" he asked with amazement.

"Chameleon assassin!" Talis looked around nervously with his sword still drawn. "You have to get out of here. This one was sent for you!"

Just then, Marie came up the road, driving a wagon. Marie called out, "Talis, Talis, chameleons have been spotted around the camp. I came to warn you. I think they're after Louie."

With noises coming from the forest behind them, Talis took Louie by the arm and pulled him to the roadside. "Hide in this wagon, go with Marie."

"But what about you?" Louie asked.

"I'll hold them off, as best I can, while you escape. Gather the troops. Tell them you're the king. Show them the picture of your father. They'll follow you. It's your turn now!" And with that, Talis ran into the open meadow, sword raised, rushing another assassin that had come out of the forest. "It falls to you Louie, it falls to you!" he called out.

Louie froze for an instant, not knowing what to do.

"Get in the wagon!" cried Marie.

Louie wanted to go and fight, to help Talis, but he obeyed Talis instead. Climbing into the wagon, Marie cracked the whip and sped off towards the blue-belly camp. Louie looked back to see Talis, surrounded by chameleons. Watching swords flashing, he saw Talis fight off several chameleons before one finally struck him from behind. As they rounded the bend, Louie saw Talis fall to the ground. Louie turned his head away as tears welled in his eyes.

As they raced into the camp, the blue-belly soldiers rushed towards their wagon.

"Where's Talis? Did you warn him?" they asked with urgency[10].

"Yes, I did. But he didn't come with us." Marie's eyes told them everything.

Leaderless, Talis' troops weren't sure what to do next. Just then a blue-belly scout came running up to the gathered soldiers. "The chameleons are moving all right. They're in all the villages saying Prince Louie is dead. And they say they've captured the blue-belly rebel leader. So now the peasant lizards who said they would join us have withdrawn. They're backing down. The chameleons have filled the peasant lizards with fear. They're not willing to fight anymore. Looks like we are on our own."

---

[10] urgency – state of being urgent - calling for immediate attention

The troops were stunned and didn't know what to do. Marie leaned over towards the back of the wagon and said, "Louie, get up." Slowly Louie emerged from beneath his cover. As he stood, all eyes turned to him. Trembling from lack of confidence, Louie was still embarrassed about his belly, which was still not blue. Nevertheless he stood, trying to overcome his fears.

As he slowly scanned the hopeful faces of these blue-belly soldiers, he heard a faint voice echoing in his head. *It falls to you Louie, it falls to you!* Louie began to fill with courage. He straightened up. Looking skyward, he yearned to hear more. Then that same small voice said, *Tell my son I love him.* Closing his eyes and taking a deep breath, he straightened up still further. Slowly, powerfully, Louie felt the strength rising up within him.

"Soldiers of my father, brave soldiers of valor[11]." Louie's voice was strong and clear. Looking them all in the eye, he continued. "I am NOT dead! And if Talis is still alive, then we must, and we will rescue him!"

The soldiers stood in awe. Stunned as well, Marie leaned over and whispered, "Louie, your belly, it's...blue." Catching light from the moon, Louie's chest had turned a magnificent, brilliant blue right before their eyes.

---

[11] valor - strength of mind or spirit that enables a person to face danger with confidence

"Wow, he really *is* the prince!" exclaimed a blue-belly soldier.

All eyes fixed on him, Louie took it all in for a moment. His transformation was complete, Louie finally knew who he was. And now he knew what to do. "We must form a plan to rescue Talis and defeat the chameleons. How many troops do we have?"

"We have barely three regiments[12] sir, just enough to form one division[13]. We were counting on the village peasants we were training to form two more divisions, but they aren't coming," replied one soldier.

"We'll get them to come." Louie smiled confidently. "But for now, three regiments will do. First, I need one regiment commander to take his regiment and head for the castle. According to our scout, the chameleons are claiming they have captured the commander, our beloved Talis. If that's true, he is still alive. We just came from the woods where Talis risked his life to save mine, so they couldn't have gone too far. If we hurry, we can catch the chameleons before they enter the castle, and rescue Talis." Turning to the first regiment commander, Louie continued. "Take your regiment and after you make the rescue, hide in the woods, outside the castle, and wait for us to join

---

[12] regiment – 729 soldiers

[13] division – 2187 soldiers

you with the other two regiments. Now go, hurry, and may you have success."

After sending off the first regiment, Louie turned to face the eager eyes of his last two regiment commanders. "Now for the fun part. Chameleons, oh sly and crafty little chameleons. They are telling the peasants I am dead. They have, no doubt, been filling these villages with lies to discourage and take the fight out of our fellow lizards. We will fight their lies with the truth, but we will be wise and skillful and bold. If we can expose the lies, reveal the truth in just the right way, we can take their minds back, and win their hearts. Here's the plan, oh, and Marie, I will need you to come with me as well."

Marie nodded her head with quiet excitement.

Louie continued. "Now I need a small platoon[14] of soldiers to dress as peasants. This platoon will be protection for Marie, and myself as we enter each village. We will start with the farthest village, and work our way towards the castle. The platoon disguised as peasants will secure the village square, and then Marie and I will reveal ourselves and shout the truth for all the villagers to hear."

"But how will you convince them? What truth will break the chameleon's hold on the peasants?" asked one of the commanders.

Reaching into his scales, Louie pulled out the

---

[14] platoon – 27 soldiers

picture. "I will show them this."

"A picture of King Scelo," sighed the commander, "Yes, that will do it."

"Marie was an eye witness to the massacre in her village. She will expose these chameleons for the bloodthirsty rulers they are. And I will show them I am still alive. And then we will identify any chameleon spies that are in their village, and take them out," Louie continued.

"But what if they try and take you out. I mean, with only a platoon for protection, they could send in troops of their own, and..." the regiment commander replied.

"That's where the rest of you come in," Louie responded. "One platoon secures the village square. The rest of the regiment surrounds and secures the entire village. The other regiment I want stationed on the outskirts of the village, between the village and the castle, where chameleon troops would come from. We will go from village to village, gathering our two missing peasant divisions. By the time we reach the first regiment, and a rescued Talis, we will be three divisions. From there we will plan our attack on the castle."

"Sounds like a good plan to me," remarked a regiment commander.

"Let's move fast. If we are quick enough, we can

be three divisions strong and outside the castle before the chameleons know what hit them. Let's move!" Louie commanded.

And with that, Louie, prince of the blue-bellies, put into motion his counter-attack against the chameleon forces in the land.

CHAPTER 14

VILLAGE TIME

Disguised as peasants, Marie and Louie, along with their platoon escort, moved into the village square. As soon as the square was secured, Louie and Marie stepped forward and began to speak. Having been under the chameleons for so long, these peasants were not used to anyone speaking so boldly in public. They began gathering around, wanting to hear what these bold lizards had to say. Knowing he didn't have much time, Louie went straight to the point. "Fellow blue-bellies, these chameleons have ruled over us for too long." This caught everyone's attention. "They are liars and will do anything to keep their power over us. They have said that if we bow to their rule, they will treat us fairly. They lie!"

Marie stood up and began telling them of the massacre of her home village. "Fellow lizards, listen to me. We were there when the chameleon general ordered all in my village to their deaths, including my father! They say they are kind rulers, but they lie! They have also told you that the prince is dead. He is NOT dead!" With that statement, Marie made way for Louie.

Pulling out the picture of King Scelo, Louie shouted, "I am Prince Louie, son of the late great king of the blue-bellies! We call all able-bodied lizards to join us, because today we will fight them, and we will win our freedom with your help." Most of the peasants, by this time, were stunned. Many nervously looked around for chameleon spies in their village. This happened in village after village. Usually at this point, the chameleons in the village would show themselves. Sometimes the spy was disguised as an ordinary peasant. He would try to discourage anyone from believing Louie. Louie would simply nod towards the spy, and his disguised platoon of troops would grab the spy and reveal his chameleon identity to the villagers. But in some villages, the spy was a high-ranking village lizard, like the mayor. At first this caught Louie by surprise, but having been around these chameleons quite a bit, he quickly recognized their ways and their curled tails.

After exposing and overcoming the chameleons in each village, the peasants became encouraged and joined Louie. As Louie and his troops got closer to the castle, his blue-belly army grew larger and stronger. In each village it became easier. Finally, at the last village, Louie and Marie gave their final speech. This time, however, there were a few more chameleon spies, and they were more aggressive. When Louie revealed his identity, three chameleons charged at him with swords drawn. It was over quickly. Two of the blue-belly platoon soldiers drew their swords and cut down two of the chameleons from behind. The third chameleon came right at Louie, thrusting his sword at Louie's chest. Louie dodged aside, avoiding the oncoming sword. He then shielded Marie and drew his sword. As the chameleon turned to face him, Louie darted away, hoping to draw the chameleon towards him, and away from Marie. When the chameleon hesitated, trying to decide whether to go after Louie or the defenseless Marie, Louie darted back towards the chameleon. With one swift swing of his sword, Louie killed the chameleon before he could make up his mind.

Marie was frozen as it all happened so quickly. Relieved and impressed, Marie asked Louie, "Where did you learn to do that?"

"Talis taught me. You didn't think we were out in that field just eating your good cooking, did you?" Louie said with a smile.

Marie smiled back. "No, I guess not."

CHAPTER 15

TREETOP ADVENTURE

Approaching the woods outside the castle, Louie met up with the advance regiment that was supposed to rescue Talis. "Where's Talis? Did you rescue him?"

"No sir, not yet. We caught the chameleon soldiers before they made it to the castle, but they have us in a stalemate. We have them surrounded here in the woods, but they have Talis, and have threatened to kill him if we move in. We're not sure what to do next. They sent a scout to get help from the castle, but we captured him before he made it. I think they're trying to wait until help arrives. They don't know that we captured their scout, but they may have sent more than one out. We're not sure," replied the soldier in charge.

Louie thought for a minute. "Okay. Here's the plan. I want the platoon that is disguised as peasants to scout the castle. See if the chameleons in the castle know what's going on yet, see if they are sending any troops this way. Be careful. I'll also need some lookout lizards to climb these high trees. If there is trouble, signal the lizards in these trees and they'll alert us here on the ground."

Looking around at his troops, Louie was pleased to know they were three divisions strong. He hoped that would be enough. "Now I need the peasant divisions to dig in on this line between us and the castle, in case the chameleon troops come from the castle. The rest of us will work on rescuing Talis."

Wanting to better understand the situation, Louie moved closer to the chameleon camp. He quickly climbed a tree. Halfway up, he could see the chameleons all in a circle with their spears ready. In the middle of their circle, was a large tree. Looking more closely, he saw Talis tied to the large tree, surrounded by chameleons. *Boy, this is going to be tough,* he thought. *How are we going to get Talis out of there alive?*

One of the things Talis taught him in their training together, was something King Scelo had taught Talis. "Whenever you need a plan, a strategy, because you're not sure what to do, take a step back. Don't panic, clear your head and stay calm. If you are standing for what's right, if you are battling evil, a thought will come to you. Direction and a plan will come as you clear your head and wait."

Louie looked skyward and closed his eyes. *Okay, clear my head. Clear my mind. How do I do that?* Louie whispered to himself. *Talis is in trouble and I have to save him. I've lost two dads in my lifetime. One I hardly knew, and my step dad who I loved very much. Talis is like a father to me. He is my last* link to my real father. I don't want to lose him... Louie's heart was full of emotion and his eyes began to fill with tears. *I need a plan to save Talis.*

Louie wiped his eyes. *This isn't working,* he thought. Then something up high in the trees caught his attention. He looked up and noticed the treetops. His heart jumped. He looked over at the large tree that held Talis. He looked up the tree, and over. Smiling, he knew he had the plan.

Louie rushed back to his troops, and said, "I need two of my best athletic lizards. One that's real light, and one who is strong, and both have to be able to climb trees very quickly and quietly."

Even as Louie spoke, it dawned on him and his troops that he was one clear choice. Without a word spoken, Louie read their thoughts. "Okay, yes. I'll be one, but who will be the other?" The blue-bellies began to look around at each other.

"What are you planning Louie," Marie stepped up and asked.

Stepping closer to Marie, Louie pointed up and said, "See the treetops? If a couple of lizards can climb these trees, I can throw the light lizard, with a rope attached to him, across to the next tree. Doing this, we can jump from tree to tree until we are in the tree that's holding Talis." Louie was getting excited because he knew this was a brilliant plan that had a good chance of working. "When you see we're safely in Talis' tree, create a distraction. Start clashing swords, making the chameleons think that their reinforcements[15] have arrived. When you draw their attention, we will climb down the tree and cut Talis free. We'll go back up the tree, hopefully unnoticed, and then you attack!"

The other lizards looked up at the treetops and understood the plan. "Brilliant, simply brilliant," remarked one older blue-belly soldier. Smiling he said, "You remind me of the old king. You really *are* his son!"

Closing his eyes, Louie let those words soak into his soul.

Taking a deep breath, he said, "So, who's going with me over these trees?"

Before anyone had a chance to speak, Marie quickly jumped in front of Louie and said, "I will."

"Marie, you can't come with me, it's too dangerous," Louie sighed.

"Who's lighter than I am? I can do this Louie, I can," she replied.

"I don't know Marie, I don't know," Louie said, shaking his head.

"She has a point Louie," the old blue-belly soldier replied. "All of us older lizards weigh too much, and the ones that don't weigh much are too young.

---

[15] reinforcements - more troops coming to help

I've seen Marie, she's strong enough all right. I think she's our best choice."

Louie nodded his head. "Okay then, let's do it," he said.

Marie and Louie, rope in hand, began climbing the first tree. When they reached the top, Louie took Marie in his strong arms and threw her across the first treetop. Landing against the side of the tree trunk with a thud, Marie groaned. She slid down until she reached a branch and caught her breath. Next she secured the rope, and Louie crawled across.

"You didn't have to throw me so hard," Marie complained, whispering loudly.

"I'm sorry. I wanted to make sure you made it across. I didn't mean to throw you so hard, are you alright?" Louie whispered with concern.

"Yeah, but ease up or I'm throwing *you* next time," she joked.

Louie smiled.

Louie and Marie continued their treetop journey, getting better with each jump. As the blue-belly troops could see their progress, they got ready for the diversion. Finally, after six successful jumps, Louie and Marie had made it to the center tree unnoticed. The blue-bellies started making noise like a battle beginning.

Hearing the clashing swords, groaning, and

mock-battle sounds, the chameleons perked up.

Slowly, Marie and Louie made their way down the tree trunk. Making sure the chameleons were all looking away, Louie gave the signal, and Marie darted down the last few feet of the tree trunk to Talis. Reaching Talis, she took out her knife and cut the ropes. Talis, sensing a rescue attempt was being made, stayed perfectly still. *Hurry Marie, hurry,* Louie thought nervously.

The blue-belly regiment leader watched with anticipation[16]. As soon as Talis was completely cut free, Marie and Talis disappeared up the tree trunk to the cover of the branches. "Attack! Attack! Attack!" the leader commanded.

Surprised and confused, the chameleons backed up towards the tree. "They're attacking us," the head chameleon shouted. "Kill the prisoner, kill the prisoner!"

Looking from the branches above, Louie, Talis and Marie loved the total surprise on the faces of the chameleons as they turned to find Talis gone. The blue-bellies moved in quickly. Having the chameleons completely outnumbered, they cut them down within minutes.

Louie and Talis hopped down from the tree, and embraced. Others quickly joined in to hug Talis and to see if he was all right. Talis was wounded, but still

---

[16] anticipation - act of looking forward

looked strong. "I think I'm going to make it," he said, as the army doctor attended to his wounds. "But I have to say, that rescue was awesome. Simply awesome!"

Louie and Marie smiled at each other, knowing that they had accomplished something very special together.

CHAPTER 16

VALOR

Leaning over Louie's shoulder, Talis said, "So what's the plan for capturing the castle, my good prince?"

Louie couldn't help but smile. "It's good to see you well, Talis. It's good to see you well." Looking up, he asked, "How do you propose we take the castle?"

"You came up with the plan to rescue me, I'm more interested in your plan," Talis replied.

"Well, I was thinking," but before Louie could finish, a voice came from the treetops.

"Scout platoon returning from the castle," the lookout lizard called out. As he turned to call back to Louie and the others, something caught the corner of his eye. He looked towards the castle to verify once again that the approaching platoon were their own troops. Then he looked back behind, in the opposite direction of the castle, to see if he really saw the movement he thought he had seen before. Staring for several seconds, he caught it again; a glimmering reflection from the sun, and some movement, coming from behind them. *Could it be?* he thought. *Could chameleon forces be coming at us from behind?* But then, he saw it again, and again; many movements and possibly swords reflecting in the sunlight.

"Chameleon forces approaching from behind! We are being attacked from behind!" he called out.

Wanting to warn Louie and Talis directly, the lookout lizard turned to climb down his tree. Then he saw more. Chameleons charging out of the castle. They were being attacked from both sides! Quickly moving down the tree, the lookout lizard found Louie and Talis together. "We are being attacked from the front and from behind, sirs!" he blurted.

Louie and Talis looked at each other and then back at this lookout lizard. Talis held himself back, allowing Louie to lead. Louie noticed Talis pause, thought for a second and then commanded. "Go back up the tree and report on anything else you see."

"Yes sir!" the lookout replied, then he ran off back to his tree.

"Talis, can you take command of the two peasant divisions facing the castle. They should hold well from your side. I'll take command of the veteran[17] division and set them up to our rear. We will fight two fronts. If you are doing well and I need help, send me some troops. But if I am doing well, and you need help, I'll send you some troops. Marie will be our runner, she will make sure our messages get through."

Talis saluted and went off to command the peasant troops facing the castle.

---

[17] veteran - old soldiers of long service and experience

Louie had to scramble the blue-belly troops quickly because they weren't expecting an attack from the rear. Fortunately Louie had command of a division of veteran blue-belly warriors that Talis had trained very well. With the help of the treetop lookouts, Louie was able to place his troops in the right positions. The chameleons thought they had caught the blue-bellies off guard, so they were surprised to find Louie and his troops waiting for them. The fighting was fierce, but the valiant[18] blue-bellies withstood attack after attack from the chameleons. Louie moved back and forth across the lines, making sure they had a complete line of defense.

Meanwhile, Talis was rallying two peasant divisions to dig in and hold the line against the chameleons attacking from the castle. He was delighted at the chance to defeat the chameleons after losing such a bitter battle twelve years ago. His strength and determination were inspiring. The peasant lizards fed off of his spirit and leadership. The chameleons tried attacking the middle first, but were thrown back. Then they tried attacking the left flank, but Talis anticipated their move and had his troops ready. Then the chameleons regrouped and tried attacking the right flank. Talis could see that the chameleons were getting frustrated. He waited for their attack on the right flank, then countered their attack. As the

---

[18] valiant – brave

chameleons threw themselves at the right, he commanded his left flank to move forward and then to the
right. As the chameleons attacked Talis' right flank,
they found themselves attacked on their right flank as
well. The chameleons became confused. They broke
off the attack in front of them and turned to face
Talis' charging troops coming at them from their
right. That was what Talis was waiting for! He waved
his signal flag, giving the entrenched troops in front of
the chameleons the command to charge. Now the
chameleons faced charging blue-belly forces from two
sides! It was too much for their exhausted troops. The
blue-bellies crushed them, cutting them down as they
tried to retreat.

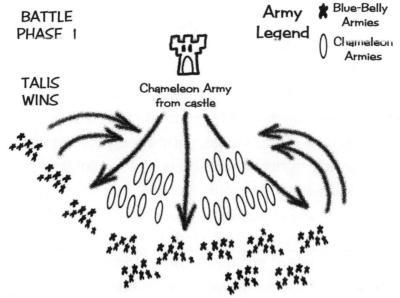

BATTLE PHASE 1

TALIS WINS

Chameleon Army from castle

Army Legend

♣ Blue-Belly Armies

◊ Chameleon Armies

Talis and Blue-Belly peasant divisions

General Cramstack was nervous. *I can't see what's going on! I need a report from the field. Did the troops sneak out of the tunnels without being seen? Did they get behind the blue-bellies and attack them quickly enough?*

Suddenly the general got his answer. A bleeding chameleon soldier ran across the field, back to the castle. General Cramstack's stomach sank. "What's your report soldier?" he barked.

"There were too many of them general. They came at us from all sides. Too many, too many," the soldier panted.

"What about the attack from behind?" the general snapped.

"Don't know, sir. I think they had five divisions, maybe more. We fell into some kind of trap. They were ready for us. They fought hard, too hard for us." The soldier faltered.

General Cramstack fumed. How could his great plan fail so miserably? He wanted satisfaction, someplace to take out his anger. "Kill him!" he commanded, pointing to the wounded chameleon soldier. The chameleon guard standing next to the general hesitated. The wounded soldier was shocked. "I said kill him!" the general commanded again. With a swift stroke, the guard cut down the wounded soldier. "Coward," the general muttered to the dead soldier.

Grabbing the guard, the general said, "Good work. Now go out into the battle, find out what's really happening, and report back. I need to know what's happened to our troops from the tunnels. Now hurry!"

The chameleon guard ran off toward the battle line.

Fighting at the rear was fierce. Louie's troops were in place, just in time. The chameleon troops had used hidden tunnels to get out of the castle and come up behind their lines. Louie's troops held their first couple of assaults, but they were outnumbered. So Louie called for Marie. "Marie, I need more troops. Find Talis and see if he can spare any at all. If he can, tell them to swing to the far left, then attack the chameleons from behind. I need these troops to close those tunnel exits. If they can take the tunnel exits, we can stop any more troops from reinforcing them."

Marie quickly ran to find Talis.

Talis was quite pleased. *These peasant soldiers have fought well,* he thought to himself. It was a total victory. Any chameleons left were running back to the castle as fast as they could run. Talis took a deep breath. It felt good to win a battle again. Then he heard a voice coming from behind him.

"Talis, Talis, can you spare some troops?" Marie

called as she approached.

"Marie, yes, how's Louie doing?" he answered.

"He's outnumbered, but holding. He needs you to send some troops to his left. He wants them to close from behind and close the tunnel exits," she replied.

Talis quickly rallied one division, minus the killed and wounded. He gave them their orders and sent them off. He then reformed his other division, organizing them in anticipation of the castle assault. Marie ran back to Louie to inform him that troops were on the way.

Louie and his troops were holding, but they were getting very tired. "How many more assaults can we withstand?" he thought out loud.

"As many as they can give!" replied a blue-belly sargent nearby.

Yes, the blue-bellies were very motivated after years of being oppressed by the chameleons. But Louie still worried if Marie had gotten through to Talis.

"Louie, Talis has sent you a division!" Marie's voice came as his answer.

Turning around to see her running up, Louie thought how good it was to hear these words. These words from this voice, the voice of his good friend,

Marie.

"Excellent," he answered. "And how is Talis doing on his front?"

"Most excellent," Marie said with a big grin. "Talis has completely destroyed the attacking army from the castle."

Louie was absolutely amazed. He knew Talis was a great commander, a great soldier, but this was better than he had hoped. Louie was filled with encouragement. "A whole division, did you say?"

"Yes! And they are going up the left flank as you requested. They should be coming in from behind the chameleons here shortly," Marie replied.

"Marie, can I get you to do one more thing for me?" Louie asked, with a look of deep thought.

"Sure, what do you need?" she asked.

"Climb up the best lookout tree you can find, take a signal flag with you. When you see Talis' troops beginning to attack the chameleons from behind, wave the flag. Then we will charge!" Louie wanted to take the chameleons out quickly and he knew this was his chance to finish them.

"Will do!" Marie replied, taking a signal flag and running towards the best lookout tree she could find.

It didn't take long before the signal from Marie came. Louie had his troops ready. When the signal came, Louie sprang up and yelled, "Charge!" He swung his sword in the air signaling his troops to follow. With a sudden surge of strength, the blue-bellies jumped up and followed Louie. Leaping over bushes and shrubs, Louie and his blue-bellies came at the chameleons at the very same time Talis' troops attacked from behind. The chameleons were confused. Louie's sword swung, hit! He moved over, and swung again. Another hit. Beside him were other blue-belly lizards striking their targets.

BATTLE PHASE 2

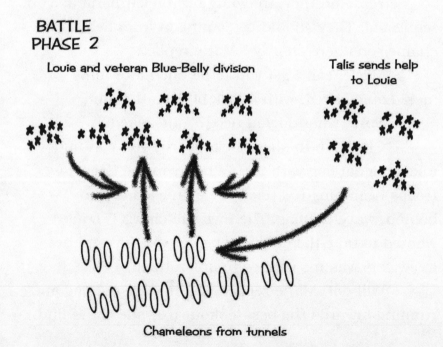

Louie and veteran Blue-Belly division

Talis sends help to Louie

Chameleons from tunnels

"Don't let up lizards," Louie called out. He wanted to strike them quickly before they could think or counterattack. Just as he yelled, a group of three chameleons dashed out of some bushes to his right. They drew their swords and charged Louie. Louie recognized them! They were the bully lizards from his school.

In this instant, time stood still. Louie remembered the alley where his brother Porez died. He realized those bully lizards were actually chameleons in disguise. *It must have been a planned ambush all along!*

With a rush of anger, Louie tucked himself tight and dove quickly at their feet. The middle chameleon tried to jump but the swinging sword from another chameleon just missed Louie and crashed into the middle chameleon's knee.

"Yeow! You got me you idiot!" yelled the middle chameleon as he fell wounded to the ground.

Louie rolled onto his feet. The two remaining chameleons turned to face him.

"Porez, this is for you," Louie said to himself. Lunging at the chameleons he swung his sword with great speed. Both chameleons backed up, holding their swords up to block Louie's strikes. One chameleon tripped over their wounded companion and Louie concentrated on the other.

Swing high, then swing low. Louie remembered his training. With the chameleon backing up, he swung his sword high for the chameleon's head. When the chameleon brought his sword up to block his blow, Louie quickly changed his swing lower and caught the chameleon square across the chest. The chameleon groaned as he went down in a heap.

Turning his attention to the last remaining chameleon, he jumped over in front of him just as he was getting back up. "Hello, remember me?" Louie said with a mocking smile. "This is for my brother!" Louie said gritting his teeth. He swung his sword hard catching the chameleon across the body.

Looking over the dead bodies of the three ex-bullies, Louie heard Marie's voice. "Louie! Watch out!"

Louie looked up and saw two large chameleons that also looked familiar. These were the other two large lizards that ambushed him and his brother that day. But these chameleons were very large and coming at him fast. Louie raised his sword just in time to block the first chameleon's swing. But the force knocked Louie backward up against a tree. Louie only had time for one thing. He ducked again and swung at the first chameleon's feet.

"Caught you," he said as he took the chameleon's feet hard with his sword. The chameleon crashed headfirst into the tree. But having done this, he was exposed to the second chameleon who was now standing over him about to swing his sword across Louie's body. Louie didn't have time to swing his sword up. He looked up into the chameleon's eyes.

Thump, came the sound. The chameleon looked at Louie and rolled his eyes and fell over. Louie was surprised until he saw the sword in the back of the chameleon.

What? Louie thought. Then he looked over and saw Marie smiling a few yards away. "Did you do that?" Louie asked with amazement.

"Yep," Marie replied.

"But how, when," Louie began.

"You think you were the only one Talis ever trained?" Marie said confidently.

Louie shook his head in respectful admiration. "You are something else, Marie, something else. Thanks."

"Your welcome, my prince," Marie said with a smile.

For the second time that day, the chameleons were completely caught off guard. Within a short while the chameleons were defeated. Talis' troops had found the tunnel exits and closed them off. The victory was almost complete.

CHAPTER 17

FOR THE LOVE OF VICTORY

The chameleon guard was very scared. Reporting bad news to the general was definitely a risk to his life. But if he ran, where would he go? Blue-bellies were everywhere. He decided to report back to the general, but he would keep his distance. Entering the castle he could see the gloom all around. The general was in a very bad mood, and no one was safe from his outbursts of anger. Just when the guard was rethinking his decision to report back, the general spotted him.

"Well, what's the news?" he snapped.

"Our forces, our forces are...gone, sir," he said, trying not to show his fear.

"Gone? Gone! How could those blue-bellies have beaten us so badly? This is impossible." The general was stunned.

Standing next to the general, Trina was more disgusted than upset. "It was that lizard massacre I bet," she said. "The massacre didn't scare them as much as it motivated them. I think that was your mistake, general."

"My mistake? My mistake? How dare you insult the supreme commander?" The general yelled, as he slapped Trina across the face. Trina tumbled back across the ground.

This was enough for the chameleon guard, he quickly slipped out of sight. As the chameleon looked to exit the castle, he noticed that the other chameleon guards had already abandoned the general and the castle. He quietly began lowering the front draw-bridge, hoping to escape before the general could find him. He started running across the drawbridge look-ing nervously behind him as he went. When he thought he was far enough along the drawbridge, he looked in front of him and suddenly stopped. Right in front of him stood Louie, Talis, Marie and the entire blue-belly army. They had the castle surrounded, and were happy to see that the drawbridge lay open for them.

Quickly moving into the castle, Louie and his forces surrounded the general, finding him in the inner court. The general was standing over a badly beaten Trina. So focused on beating her, the general didn't notice Louie's presence until he spoke.

"Stop general! Surrender now!" Louie command-ed with authority. Louie had been overjoyed at the extent of the blue-belly victory, but when he saw the general he remembered. He remembered how cruel these chameleons could be. He remembered his pain, the loss of his fathers, the massacre of Marie's village, and he remembered his dad, the king. As though he were going back in time, twelve plus years, in this very castle, clear memories flooded his mind; his father, the king, holding him, playing with him, loving him. As a rush of emotion overcame him, he broke out of the vision with a deep determination.

"Surrender now, or die!" Louie called to the general.

The general seemed to know what Louie was thinking, because he turned away from Trina and smiled. "You and me, little lizard?" he said with a motion of his eyebrows.

"No Louie, don't," Marie pleaded, putting her hand on his arm.

Talis put his hand on Marie's, and gently removed it from Louie's arm. "Louie will be fine, Marie. He has to do this."

Marie looked into Talis' eyes. She did not understand, but trusting Talis, she let go of Louie's arm.

Louie didn't feel any fear. For the first time in his life, he understood. He knew what gave the chameleons power. He knew they fed on other lizard's fear. If he was not afraid, the general could not defeat him. And Louie also knew he had to demonstrate this courage to the rest of his blue-bellies, so they all could learn not to fear the chameleons and their lying

ways.

General Cramstack drew his sword, then he disappeared. Marie gasped. Louie knew he was not gone, simply camouflaged. Staying calm, Louie took a deep breath and drew his sword as well. He looked down at the dirt floor. Ah, he could see them, the imprints of the general's feet. The general had not moved. Louie made it seem like he didn't know where the general was. He moved wildly to his left, then to his right, pretending to show fear. The footsteps in the dirt started to move. Louie held still, sensing the general's next move. Then...Louie dove to his right. Clang! The general's sword swung where Louie used to be. Louie rolled, popped up and swung his sword. Thwack! A direct hit, Louie caught the general in his right shoulder. Color came back into the chameleon as the general staggered, holding his shoulder. "You think you can take me, little lizard, do you?" taunted the general.

"I can take you and I will take you. You dirty counterfeit[19] lizard," replied Louie.

"Concentrate, concentrate," Talis muttered under his breath. "Don't let him distract you."

"I killed your father. Ha, both of them. And I will kill you too," responded the general as he disappeared under his camouflage again.

Louie looked down again, trying to find the gen-

---

[19] counterfeit – made to look real but false

eral's footprints. This time he saw them almost too late. The general rushed at him. Louie ducked just in time. Swoosh came the general's sword. Louie whipped his tail low and curled it around the general's feet, then he yanked. The general came crashing down, and again his color came back.

Louie jumped to his feet and quickly raised his sword with both hands and hit Cramstack right down the middle of his back. "You also killed my brother and Marie's father," Louie said as he stood over the limp body of the general. Louie started to lower his sword when the general rolled and swung his sword at Louie's head.

Clang! Louie barely blocked the blow.

The general was wounded and bleeding but he still had some strength.

Now change it up. Swing low then swing high, Louie thought quickly. *Time to finish him.*

Louie began swinging his sword low across the general's knees. As the general moved his sword to block him, Louie quickly swung high. Swoosh! Louie caught the general good. The general staggered and fell.

The blue-bellies, relieved and amazed, cheered loudly. "Lou-eee! Lou-eee! Lou-eee!"

Marie was so relieved she couldn't contain herself. She rushed to Louie and gave him a big hug, burying her head into his chest. Marie quietly cried. Louie held her and slowly began to understand. All the years of chameleon oppression, the village massacre, losing her father, and now it was finally over. Louie stroked her little lizard face, and wiped a tear from her eye.

Meanwhile, a couple of blue-belly soldiers picked Trina up, intending to put her into prison. As she passed by Louie, Trina motioned to the soldiers and turned to Louie. "I always knew you would make a great king some day."

"Yes, just not the kind of king you were expecting," Louie said as he managed a half-smile in her direction.

The soldiers tried to move her on, but Trina wanted to say something more. "Louie, I'm sorry for trying to make you into a chameleon king. You were meant to be the blue-belly king, and I believe these blue-bellies will be the better for it."

"And I hope someday you will realize there are things more important than power," Louie replied hopefully.

Trina nodded her head. "Yes, maybe someday," she said as the soldiers took her off to prison.

Looking up at Louie, Marie asked, "Do you think she will ever get it, Louie?"

"I don't know Marie, I really don't know," Louie

replied. "But you know, she does have a point."

Marie looked at him curiously.

"She said I will make a great blue-belly king, and you know that beside every great king there needs to be a great queen," Louie said, smiling broadly at Marie.

Shocked, Marie backed away from Louie. "Are you asking me to marry you?"

Quickly getting down on one knee, Louie took Marie's hand. "Will you marry me and be my queen?"

Marie put her hand to her throat and gasped.

"I'll even promise never to throw you too hard against a tree, ever again!" Louie said with a big grin.

Marie laughed. "Yes. Yes. I'll marry you."

Louie rose to his feet and hugged Marie as the other blue-bellies began congratulating them. Talis embraced them both. The blue-bellies continued with their celebration as they hugged each other and danced around with silly joy. Soon all the villages in the land heard the good news. Blue-bellies from all around streamed to the castle as the victory party lasted throughout the night and into the next morning.

And so, the kingdom was established under King Louie and Queen Marie. Talis once again became the army commander for the blue-belly king. They were able to rid the land of chameleons and free the blue-belly villagers from their cruelty. The blue-belly lizards of the land grew stronger than ever before. And lastly, King Louie took all the knowledge he and the others had learned from battling the chameleons and established a school of wisdom. A school that would teach future generations how to expose and fight chameleon lies, so blue-belly lizards would not fall under the cruel power of chameleons, ever again.

STUDY GUIDE

DIRECTIONS:
VOCABULARY: Look up the bold-faced vocabulary words using a
dictionary to find the definitions or a thesaurus to find the synonyms.

COMPREHENSIVE QUESTIONS: Answer the questions relating to each
chapter.

CHAPTER 1 – ANGRY KOMODO DRAGON
VOCABULARY:
1. You broke the treaty, my trust, and our friendship...and all to assure
your son would rule this island **unchallenged**.
2. The King thoughts raced as he watched his own warrior's **futile**
attempt to hold Komo back.
3. In a moment, in a vision flashing through his mind; **assassins** coming in at night, catching the young monitor lizard asleep.

COMPREHENSIVE QUESTIONS:
1. Why did King Scelo send Talis back to the castle?
2. How were the chameleons able to defeat the blue-belly army?

CHAPTER 2 – NEW PLANS
VOCABULARY:
1. But from behind some bushes came a **tattered** soldier.
2. Later that day, after nursing their wounds and collecting a few more
stragglers, Talis laid out the plan.
3. "Yes! And when the time is right, we will **reclaim** this land in the
name of the King and free the common lizards from the chameleon cruelty!"
4. "Yes, if we can **convert** him into a chameleon prince, then he can be
our little puppet King, all the appearance of a real King, but without
any power.
5. It would **secure** our hold on this land for a good long time," the general said with pleasure.

COMPREHENSIVE QUESTIONS:
1. What was the good news that the blue-belly soldier gave Talis in the
woods?
2. How did Talis decide to hide Louie from the chameleons?

CHAPTER 3 – COMMON LIZARD
VOCABULARY:
1. However, the chameleons were masters at **maintaining** their control over the land.
2. But slowly Louie became **convinced** that there was something wrong about this lizard.
3. The chief spy responded, "He **assumed** the **identity** of a peasant lizard, as we came to suspect.
4. A ten-year-old without a dad, yes, that will make him **defenseless** to our powers.
5. Then I want as much mistreatment as you can **generate** towards him.

COMPREHENSIVE QUESTIONS:
1. Who was making plans to have bad things happen to Louie and his family?
2. Why do you think it took so long for the chameleons to find Louie?

CHAPTER 4 – ROUGH TIMES
VOCABULARY:
1. Louie was overcome with grief and the incredible **stress** of knowing he was now the head of the house.
2. The friendly lizard made sure the **pursuing** lizards saw him and then he disappeared, running around the corner.

COMPREHENSIVE QUESTIONS:
1. Name two bad things that happened to Louie?
2. Who did the lizard behind the fence think Louie was?

CHAPTER 5 – TRINA
VOCABULARY:
1. As far as he could tell, many a poor male lizard was left humiliated and **distressed** by his unsuccessful **attempts** to **obtain** the friendship and **affection** of the pretty little female lizards.
2. But Trina was a **determined** lizard and Louie was a challenge.

COMPREHENSIVE QUESTIONS:
1. Did Louie feel like he knew Trina very well? Why?
2. Who wanted to meet Louie in the field at midnight? Why?

CHAPTER 6 – CASTLE CLUES
VOCABULARY:
1. He went to a bookshelf and **scanned** the titles.
2. The only time the two guards weren't **hovering** over him was when he was in a room with Trina.
3. "If this is the life of a prince, then I'm not interested!" Louie said with growing **boldness**.
4. "Tomorrow we will go into the villages and I'll teach you how to rule," the general stated **blandly** as he burst into the room with Trina on his heels.

COMPREHENSIVE QUESTIONS:
1. What did the chameleons want to do with Louie?
2. What did Louie find in the library?

CHAPTER 7 – CHAMELEON POWER
VOCABULARY:
1. Cramstack **regained** his feet and drew his sword.
2. Like these **peasant** lizards had something he didn't have.
3. "What?" Louie said, still getting over the shock of the **massacre**.
4. "I am? I'm a chameleon? Are you sure?" Louie said **skeptically**.

COMPREHENSIVE QUESTIONS:
1. Who saved Marie's life?
2. Why didn't the birds see Louie in the field along with the other lizards?

CHAPTER 8 – FOREST DREAM
VOCABULARY:
1. Louie quickly **scampered** up the tree and breathed a huge sigh of relief.
2. Louie climbed out of the bushes and as he **approached** them their laughter just increased.
3. The **suspended** lizard looked him right in the eye and said, "You are the prince!"
4. He walked **cautiously** passed several gathered lizards but they simply nodded to him without much notice.

COMPREHENSIVE QUESTIONS:
1. Why did the lizards laugh at Louie in his dream?
2. Who found Louie in the woods?

CHAPTER 9 – NEW BEGINNING
VOCABULARY:
1. First, as soon as the chameleons gather themselves and realize we have Louie, they will seek **revenge** on his family.
2. I want to bring him to this **realization** slowly, but I need your help.
3. As long as it takes, I need you all to treat him just like an **ordinary** lizard.
4. "We don't," replied Talis **somberly**.
5. But being curious and **anxious** for answers, Louie did what he was told and followed Talis into the forest.
6. And in between the physical lessons, Talis taught Louie wisdom in how to rule the lizards with fairness and **mercy**.

COMPREHENSIVE QUESTIONS:
1. When Louie asked if he was a blue-belly lizard or if he was a chameleon, did Talis tell him?
2. Talis started training Louie, for what?

CHAPTER 10 – ANGRY CHAMELEONS
VOCABULARY:
1. How could you **bumbling** idiots lose the prince?
2. And it would be very sad if Trina lost her prince, now wouldn't it?" **sneered** Cramstack.

COMPREHENSIVE QUESTIONS:
1. What were the chameleons afraid Louie might discover?
2. Why didn't Trina care if Louie was killed?

CHAPTER 11 – WHO AM I?
VOCABULARY:
1. But Marie never showed any **bitterness** towards him, even though Louie knew she had lost many friends that day, maybe even family members.
2. "You were up there and it looked like you had the **authority** to stop what I knew was going to be a massacre," Marie answered.

COMPREHENSIVE QUESTIONS:
1. While speaking with Louie, what did Marie need to know?
2. Where did Louie catch the spirit of courage, according to Marie?

CHAPTER 12 – IT FALLS TO ME

VOCABULARY:
1. Talis saw an increase in **maturity.**
2. "Have you decided what you want to be or, more **accurately**, *who* you want to be?" Talis asked him.
3. Could it be, after so many years of being so lost and confused, he was finally **grasping** who he really was?
4. He then told Louie of that **fateful** day, when through lies and trickery, the chameleons killed his father, and took the land.
5. How his father, the king, had outsmarted his enemies with **superior** strategy and tactics.

COMPREHENSIVE QUESTIONS:
1. Who is Louie's father?
2. What type of special deception defeated Louie's father?

CHAPTER 13 – DESTINY

VOCABULARY:
1. **Trembling** from **lack** of confidence, Louie was still embarrassed about his belly, which was still not blue.

COMPREHENSIVE QUESTIONS:
1. Who risked his life so Louie could escape?
2. What happened to Louie right after he stood up and spoke to the blue-belly soldiers?

CHAPTER 14 – VILLAGE TIME

VOCABULARY:
1. After **exposing** and **overcoming** the chameleons in each village, the peasants became encouraged and joined Louie.
2. **Relieved** and impressed, Marie asked Louie, "Where did you learn to do that?"

COMPREHENSIVE QUESTIONS:
1. How did Louie, Marie and the blue-bellies disguise themselves?
2. What did Louie do that impressed Marie so much?

CHAPTER 15 - TREETOP ADVENTURE
VOCABULARY:
1. Louie's heart was full of **emotion** and his eyes began to fill with tears.
2. As the blue-belly troops could see their progress, they got ready for the **diversion**.
3. Talis, **sensing** a rescue attempt was being made, stayed perfectly still.

COMPREHENSIVE QUESTIONS:
1. Who was the perfect choice to help Louie rescue Talis?
2. What were the surrounded chameleons going to do if the blue-bellies attacked?

CHAPTER 16 - VALOR
VOCABULARY:
1. Starring for several seconds, he caught it again; a **glimmering** reflection from the sun, and some movement, coming from behind them.
2. We will fight two **fronts**.
3. Marie will be our **runner**, she will make sure our messages get through.
4. Then they tried attacking the left flank, but Talis **anticipated** their move and had his troops ready.
5. Then the chameleons **regrouped** and tried attacking the right flank.
6. He waved his signal flag, giving the **entrenched** troops in front of the chameleons the command to charge.
7. The soldier **faltered**.
8. *It must have been a planned* **ambush** *all along!*
9. **Lunging** at the chameleons he swung his sword with great speed.

COMPREHENSIVE QUESTIONS:
1. How did the chameleons get behind Louie and his army?
2. As Louie fought the bully chameleons, who saved Louie's life?

CHAPTER 17 - FOR THE LOVE OF VICTORY
VOCABULARY:
1. How dare you **insult** the supreme commander?
2. Meanwhile, a couple of blue-belly soldiers picked Trina up, **intending** to put her into prison.

COMPREHENSIVE QUESTIONS:
1. Who killed General Cramstack?
2. Who became King Louie's queen?

Chapter 1

Vocabulary:
1. unchallenged: without any trouble or resistance
2. futile: useless
3. assassins: a murderer who kills quickly by surprise

Comprehension:
1. King Scelo sent Talis back to the castle to get Louie.
2. The chameleons were able to defeat the blue-belly army because they had Komo the monitor lizard fighting with them.

Chapter 2

Vocabulary:
1. tattered; torn: ragged
2. stragglers: people arriving at different times; slowpokes
3. reclaim: to demand the return of
4. convert: to change
5. secure: to protect

Comprehension:
1. The good news was that the chameleons didn't have the komodo dragon anymore.
2. Talis hid Louie from the chameleons by putting him with a peasant family.

Chapter 3

Vocabulary:
1. maintaining; keeping
2. convinced: to become certain
3. assumed: put on identity; likeness
4. defenseless: helpless
5. generate; make; bring about

Comprehension:
1. General Cramstack was making plans to have bad things happen to Louie and his family.
2. It took so long for the chameleons to find Louie because he was disguised as a peasant.

Chapter 4

Vocabulary:
1. stress: pressure
2. pursuing: searching

Comprehension:
1. Two bad things that happened to Louie were the death of his dad and brother.
2. The lizard behind the fence thought Louie was a prince.

Chapter 5

Vocabulary:
1. distressed: worried
   attempts: to give a try
   obtain: to get
   affection: love; attention
2. determined: having one's mind made up

Comprehension:
1. No, Louie didn't feel like he knew Trina very well because she never talked about herself.
2. Trina wanted to meet Louie in the field at midnight to meet her friends.

Chapter 6

Vocabulary:
1. scanned: to look at quickly
2. hovering: waiting close by
3. boldness: bravery
4. blandly: without feeling

Comprehension:
1. The chameleons wanted to make Louie their prince.
2. Louie found a picture of a blue-belly king in the library.

Chapter 7

Vocabulary:
1. regained: to get back
2. peasant: a person of the class of farm workers
3. massacre: the act of killing a large number of people
4. skeptically: not believing; doubtful

Comprehension:
1. Marie's dad saved Marie's life.
2. The birds didn't see Louie in the field along with the other lizards because the chameleons put a camouflaged blanket over him.

Chapter 8

Vocabulary:
1. scampered: to run
2. approached: to come near
3. suspended: to hang
4. cautiously: carefully

Comprehension:
1. The lizards in Louie's dream laughed at him because he thought he was a chameleon.
2. Marie found Louie in the woods.

Chapter 9

Vocabulary:
1. revenge: to get someone back for hurt
2. realization: thinking; understanding
3. ordinary: normal; common
4. somberly: gloomy
5. anxiously: impatient; not able to wait
6. mercy: kindness

Comprehension:
1. Talis didn't tell Louie when Louie asked if he was a blue-belly lizard or if he was a chameleon. He answered with a question instead.
2. Talis started training Louie to be a good king.

Chapter 10

Vocabulary:
1. bumbling: clumsy
2. sneered: smirk

Comprehension:
1. The chameleons were afraid Louie might discover he was the blue-belly prince.
2. Trina didn't care if Louie was killed because then she would get a new prince.

Chapter 11

Vocabulary:
1. bitterness: harshness
2. authority: power; control

Comprehension:
1. Marie needed to know if Louie could have prevented her dad from getting killed.
2. Marie believed Louie caught the spirit of courage from her dad.

Chapter 12

Vocabulary:
1. maturity: to grow up
2. accurately: right; exact
3. grasping: to hold onto
4. fateful: important happening or event
5. superior: being above the level of another

Comprehension:
1. King Scelo is Louie's father.
2. *Chameleon* deception defeated Louie's father.

Chapter 13

Vocabulary:
1. trembling: shaking
   lack: not having enough

Comprehension:
1. Talis risked his life so Louie could escape.
2. Right after Louie stood up and spoke to the blue-belly soldiers his belly turned blue.

Chapter 14

Vocabulary:
1. exposing: allowing to be seen
   overcoming: to win; to beat
2. relieved: to lighten

Comprehension:
1. Louie, Marie and the blue-bellies disguised themselves as peasants.
2. Louie impressed Marie when he killed the attacking chameleon.

Chapter 15

Vocabulary:
1. emotion: feeling
2. diversion: distraction; to turn away one's attention in another direction
3. sensing: knowing; understanding

Comprehension:
1. Marie was the perfect choice to help Louie rescue Talis.
2. If the blue-bellies attacked, the surrounded chameleons were going to kill Talis.

Chapter 16

Vocabulary:
1. glimmering: sparkle
2. fronts: a place where soldiers meet the enemy
3. runner: a person who carries information between two people
4. anticipated: one step ahead of
5. regrouped: to get together again
6. entrenched: settled
7. faltered: stumble; wobble
8. ambush: to trap an enemy by lying in hiding until a surprise attack can be made
9. lunging: drive forward

Comprehension:
1. The chameleons used tunnels to get behind Louie and his army.
2. Marie saved Louie's life as he fought the bully chameleons.

Chapter 17

Vocabulary:
1. insult: to speak with disrespect
2. intending: to mean; to purpose

Comprehension:
1. Louie killed General Cramstack.
2. Marie became King Louie's queen.